The crossing beam lowered in front of the tracks and Oz slowed the SUV to a stop.

The rev of a loud engine caused Oz to look in the rearview mirror. A large truck barreled toward their SUV, not slowing down for the crossing.

The truck slammed into the rear of their car. Metal crunched and flung Oz's body into the steering wheel. The rear compartment crushed into the back seat. Brute force from the truck pushed them onto the tracks. The train gained ground toward the crossing and blared the horn as a warning.

Oz turned the key in the ignition, but the car wouldn't crank. With each attempt, the train sped closer.

"Get out." Oz unbuckled his belt.

Liz grabbed her seat belt and tugged. "It's stuck."

He pressed the release and pulled. No movement.

The red engine barreled forward and air brakes squealed their effort to stop, but with all the weighted cars pushing the locomotive down the tracks, the engineer would never be able to avoid impact.

If they didn't get out now, they'd both die.

Shannon Redmon remembers the first book she checked out from the neighborhood bookmobile, sparking her love of stories. She hopes to immerse readers into a world of faith, hope and love, all from the beautiful scenery of her North Carolina mountain home, where she lives with her amazing husband, two boys and white foo-foo dog named Sophie. Connect with Shannon on Twitter @shannon_redmon or visit her online at www.shannonredmon.com.

Books by Shannon Redmon

Love Inspired Suspense

Cave of Secrets
Secrets Left Behind
Mistaken Mountain Abduction
Christmas Murder Cover-Up

Visit the Author Profile page at LoveInspired.com.

CHRISTMAS MURDER COVER-UP

SHANNON REDMON

LOVE INSPIRED SUSPENSE
INSPIRATIONAL ROMANCE

LOVE INSPIRED® SUSPENSE
INSPIRATIONAL ROMANCE

Recycling programs
for this product may
not exist in your area.

ISBN-13: 978-1-335-59767-0

Christmas Murder Cover-Up

For questions and comments about the quality of this book, please contact us
at CustomerService@Harlequin.com.

Love Inspired
22 Adelaide St. West, 41st Floor
Toronto, Ontario M5H 4E3, Canada
www.LoveInspired.com

Printed in U.S.A.

For if ye forgive men their trespasses,
your heavenly Father will also forgive you.
—*Matthew* 6:14

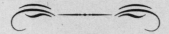

To my mother and sister—
thank you for all your support in my writing and
for being strong women of faith who live their lives for
Jesus. I dedicate this book to you with all my love.

ONE

White frost edged the third-floor window as Narcotics Detective Liz Burke scanned the parking lot below for unwanted visitors. No stray cars lingered outside her confidential informant's apartment, and the only person near the building was one homeless man tucked into an alcove of a neighboring gas station across the street. He hadn't moved in the last two hours, and Liz wondered if he was alive. She pulled out her phone and called Dispatch for a wellness check.

Other than a stray cat roaming the streets for his next meal, all seemed to be quiet, which made her nervous. Quiet always preceded the storms in her life. Things would be going well, and then out of nowhere, tragedy struck. A trait she shared with Tillie, the young woman who called an hour ago, frantic about death threats and being followed.

The nineteen-year-old sat on the couch, socked feet tucked underneath her, and fumbled with a hair tie securing her long dark braid as she scrolled on her cell.

Liz let the blinds snap closed and crossed the living room, holding out her hand. "Phone."

With an eye roll, Tillie surrendered the glittery pink

device. "Do you really have to check everything? Feels a little like prison again."

"In prison you didn't get a phone, and I'm swapping this one out in case you're being tracked. If someone really is planning to kill you, then we can't take any chances."

"You don't believe me?"

"Doesn't matter if I believe you or not. I'm here to protect you from any threat, real or false." Liz pulled another burner phone from her pocket and held the device out for Tillie to take. "Only me, your counselor and your father, okay?"

"Fine." The girl went back to scrolling, and Liz placed the other phone on the kitchen island. She'd have the security team run diagnostics in the morning. Maybe they could get a lead on the threat before anyone got hurt. "Who told you about the hit?"

"My friend Clive." The woman scratched her little brown dog's head and he nuzzled into her lap. "He heard it through one of his connections. He's really worried, and Clive's not the kind of guy who gets worried."

"The leader of the East Mountain Mafia? He's dangerous, Tillie."

"Yeah, but he's the one with the good information I share with you. Besides, he likes me, and sometimes that works in my favor." A dreamy look crossed her face.

Liz bit back the parent lecture rising to her tongue. She hadn't listened at Tillie's age in regard to the kind of men her mother wanted her to date. Boy, was that a mistake. Instead, Liz dug for more information. "Did he say who was going to carry out the hit?"

"He didn't give me a name. I don't think he knew

who exactly, but he said he heard about the threat from a reliable source." Tillie adjusted the dog's crystal-encrusted collar. "And he said it would be a professional. You can stop them, right?"

The dreaded question always placed Liz in a difficult spot. She didn't want to lie, but she couldn't promise they wouldn't get hurt either. "I'll do everything in my power to protect you."

And she would—despite the fact that Tillie was getting her narcotics information from Clive Hawkins, the leader of the East Mountain Mafia. Not the first time the man's name crossed Liz's path. The gang was one of the most dangerous in the area. She wasn't sure why the man liked Tillie so much, but maybe that would play in their favor.

Clive associated with some of the most vile people despite his recent claims of legitimizing his business ventures. They were all fronts for drug trafficking, money laundering and any other venture, earning a large payout. If Liz played her cards right, then perhaps she could stop an assassin, expose the man's criminal behavior and throw him in prison for a long time to come. Tillie might not see the wolf in sheep's clothing that he was, but Liz wouldn't underestimate him.

Now was a good time to set up Tillie in witness protection. Liz had put the move off long enough in hopes of gaining more credible information, but with this viable threat hanging over Tillie's head, Liz couldn't wait any longer.

She scrolled through her phone and tapped her contact at WITSEC. When he didn't pick up, she left a voice mail, then scanned the outside area again.

"I'm sorry, Tillie. Maybe being my confidential informant isn't a good idea anymore."

"Are you kidding me? We're so close to finding out who's pulling the strings in this area, and we've stopped a lot of people from getting hurt."

"I can't let you continue when your life is in danger."

"Please don't take me off this case. It's the only way I can make things right with my father for all the damage I did when I was addicted. You helped me get clean and my life is better now. I'm going to study criminology all because of you."

Liz crossed the room and took a seat next to the young woman. "I'm so glad to hear of your plans, and I'll give you a reference for whatever school you decide to attend. We wouldn't have been able to stop as much of the trafficking without the information you provided. You've done a good job for us, and I'm grateful."

"But...?"

"But it's time to pull you out."

With all of Tillie's intel, Liz had been able to construct a list of names, locations and networks, allowing them to shut down at least three operations, but their job was never done. When one cartel was removed from the streets, another stepped in to pick up where they left off, thinking they would be more clever. The battle to rid the area of heroin and opioids never stopped.

Liz thought of Tillie as more like a little sister or friend than an informant, but with the threats on her life, she had no other choice but to put her into protective custody. She'd miss working with her, but if Tillie could return to school and get an education in another part of the country, that would be worth letting her go. Liz wasn't sure how Tillie would take the news of going into witness protection, especially if she had to leave her father.

"We'll get you to a safe house until we have more information on who's behind the threat, and then we're going to have to put you into protective custody for a while. I've contacted WITSEC."

Tillie's head popped up. "No, Liz. I don't want to have to give up my life here."

"We talked about this. If your cover's been blown and you stay, then your life is in danger. Let's find a school in another city for you to attend and study. Maybe somewhere on the West Coast and under a different name, of course."

Tillie grabbed Liz's hand. "Maybe Clive was wrong. He's always confusing the details. The hit could be for someone else."

Liz didn't respond. Clive didn't get his facts wrong and Tillie knew it. Liz couldn't demand the move since the young woman had to volunteer to go, but this was the only way to keep the girl safe right now.

"I wouldn't be able to see my father or my friends." Tears welled up in Tillie's eyes.

"You haven't seen him in two years. He doesn't know where you are or if you're alive. Why the sudden desire to reconnect?"

"I've always hoped, after I completed my work with you, that we'd be able to patch things up. He's a good man, and I want to apologize for all I put him through."

"I'll see if we can arrange a meeting before you go, but once you enter WITSEC, we have to cut all ties with your life here."

Tillie planted a kiss on the dog's head and changed the subject. "If we could delay that decision for a while,

I'd be grateful. You can keep me safe until then, right? Maybe I could hire a private security guard."

"With what money?"

Her eyes teared up again. "At least I have my sweet Mocha. She does get to come with me, right?"

Liz hated to keep disappointing the woman, but she had to be truthful. "Unfortunately, no."

"Then forget it. I'm not going anywhere without my dog."

She should've known her efforts to persuade Tillie to enter witness protection depended on her pet. "We could get you another one, not exactly like Mocha but another breed."

"No, thanks. I'll figure something else out."

Liz stood and glanced at her watch in frustration. Maybe with a bit more time, Tillie would see the wisdom of disappearing for a while. No sense in arguing about it right now when the marshal hadn't even called her back.

She walked to the window again and stared at the lighted Christmas tree in the middle of the courtyard. Her cousin's annual Christmas party had started thirty minutes ago. Looked like she wasn't going to make the event, but her informant's safety came first. "I need to make another call, then I'll whip us up some dinner, and we can find a movie or something to watch. We can discuss witness protection again later after you've had some time to process everything."

Tillie motioned toward the kitchen. "We'll have to order takeout. My fridge is empty, and I usually grab something at the local market on my way home, but I was so spooked I ran most of the way here and locked myself inside. Mocha hasn't had anything to eat either and we're famished."

She held up her little dog and moved his paw over his tummy. Liz smiled at the gesture, tapped her cousin's number and texted her a message regarding her absence. "How close is the local market?"

"At the corner. Really close."

"Fine. I'll run down, pick up something to eat and get some dog food, but you can't open the door for anyone until I get back, okay?"

"Mocha and I will be fine, and I promise to keep the door locked while you're gone."

"Perfect." Liz slipped on her coat. "Keep the new cell with you, and I'll be back in fifteen minutes. No one gets inside until you hear my voice. Got it?"

Tillie stood, placed the dog on one of the decorative pillows and gave a small salute. "Yes, ma'am."

Liz grabbed her gun, securing it in her shoulder holster and fastened her badge to her belt. With a quick step forward, Tillie wrapped Liz in an unexpected hug. "Thanks for coming. I feel better knowing you're here until we can figure out what to do. I'm so sorry to ruin your plans for the night."

"You didn't ruin my plans."

"You're all dressed up, your hair is curled and you're wearing red lipstick. If that doesn't scream night out, then I don't know what does."

Liz didn't consider dark jeans, black boots and a red silky top as dressy, but Tillie had only witnessed her work look—minimal makeup and a ponytail. "I had a Christmas party to attend, but you're my first priority, and I'm not going to let anything happen to you."

"Thanks."

"When I get back, will you at least talk to my contact at WITSEC? He can tell you more about the program. Entering might be the only way to keep you alive, and they have an amazing record of keeping people safe."

"I'm not making any promises, and I want to talk to my dad before I make a decision."

"That can be arranged."

Liz understood the reservations that came with moving to a new place. Two years ago, she left Charlotte, North Carolina, and came to Mills Creek, looking for a pine-scented refuge from her past. Something about the strength of the mountains and the people who lived here comforted her soul. Maybe it was the guns in their trucks, the flags in their yards or the church bells on Sunday mornings that made her feel at home. God brought her to this safe haven, and so far she hadn't regretted the decision.

"I'll be back in fifteen minutes." Liz stepped into the hallway.

"I'll be waiting."

Tillie closed the door, and the click of the dead bolt engaged. Liz headed for the stairs and walked a block to the local market. The small shop wasn't as big as a grocery store chain but carried the essentials.

After purchasing a couple of frozen pizzas, one quart of ice cream and twelve ounces of dog food, Liz paid for her items and headed back into Tillie's frozen neighborhood. Storefronts boasted decorative lights and happy holiday greetings on their windows. Christmas music floated out to meet her as she passed by, an enticement to enter and spend her hard-earned money. Instead, she kept walking toward the apartment building. A cold wind blew, and Liz pulled her coat over her head as her phone rang.

"You can't text me and tell me you aren't coming without more details. What's keeping you from the best Christmas party of the season?" Her cousin Aggie, a former helicopter pilot for the military, had moved back home several years ago to help her mother on their family's apple farm.

The place was a beautiful retreat, and Liz loved to visit, but with her current situation, she had to remain with Tillie.

"I'm sorry. Something came up, and I have to take care of it. You know how work goes sometimes."

Her cousin was married to Bronson Young, one of Mills Creek's best homicide detectives. That group always got called out during the most inconvenient times. She was sure Aggie understood.

"I do know and figured it was a work thing. No worries. We already have a record crowd here at the apple farm tonight, but we'll miss you for sure. I'll keep some of Mom's pie for you."

"That would be great. Thanks for understanding."

"Your ex isn't causing problems again, is he?"

Liz didn't want to talk about Trey McManus anymore. She'd wasted two years on the man and sacrificed her home just to get away. He wasn't going to steal her joy this Christmas season. She loved her cousin Aggie, and if she and Bronson had not intervened, Liz wasn't sure she'd be alive right now.

"Of course not. I'd tell you if he was."

Never again would she be a victim. In fact, she liked living on her own. Something she'd learned about herself with her move to Mills Creek.

A cold wind blew against her face, and she pulled the bag closer to her body, wishing she'd remembered to put on her gloves. Instead, she quickened her pace and pulled open the door to Tillie's building.

Heat wrapped around her as she entered the lobby and took the stairs. "Trey's out of my life for good. Long gone. I just hope he learned his lesson."

"He better have or Bronson will make his life miserable."

Liz kept climbing the steps—an aerobic workout for sure. The building had an elevator, but she hated small spaces and always took the stairs. "My confidential informant is having a crisis, and I'm at her apartment. I need to make sure she's safe."

"That doesn't sound good."

"It's an emergency, and the extenuating circumstance can't wait. I have to help her."

"We girls have to stick together," Aggie said as Christmas music played in the background.

"Sounds like things are cranking up there. I'll call you tomorrow and see how everything went." Liz reached the third-floor landing, then stepped into the corridor. "Tell your mom—"

She stopped. A chill ran up her arms. High-pitched barks echoed off the walls. She'd recognize that yap anywhere.

"Tell my mom what?"

Liz placed her bags on the floor and removed her gun. "I've gotta go."

"Everything okay?"

"I'm not sure."

"Want me to send Bronson over?"

She leaned close to the wall and surveyed the hallway. All the neighbors' doors were closed, but a sliver of light streaked across the dirty carpet near the end. Right outside Tillie's apartment. Her door was ajar.

"Let me call you back." Liz dropped her phone into her coat pocket and approached with caution.

Two gunshots fired.

She ran the remaining length of the hallway and entered through the broken casing with her weapon aimed. Mocha stood at the back windows barking. Liz rounded the couch and found her informant's body. Tillie's blood stained the hardwood floors.

She pressed two fingers against the young woman's neck out of habit. Of course, there was no pulse, not with fatal bullet wounds to the head and chest. Tillie's skin was still warm to the touch. Liz had promised to keep her safe. She should've acted sooner and pulled her informant out while they still had time to get her to a safe place.

Tillie was right. Someone had hired a professional to take her out, and if Liz were honest, she'd doubted the story. Several of her informants embellished threats for attention or because they were lonely and wanted company. Not the case with Tillie.

A noise thumped from the bedroom. Liz rose and moved through the rest of the space, clearing the kitchen and hallway closet on her way to the primary suite. She slowed her steps as she approached the door and stepped onto the carpet.

A large man, dressed in dark clothes, bolted from the shadows, knocked the gun from her hand and skidded the weapon under a dresser, out of reach.

Liz turned, ready for his attack. He swung. Pain coursed through her arms when she blocked his barrage of hits and fought back, using every Krav Maga skill she'd mastered, but the man was stronger.

Another strike to her face shot stars through her vision. The taste of blood coated her tongue, and her eyes watered with every blow. She couldn't see to fight back. Not the first time she'd taken a beating.

A piercing tone rang through her ears. Visions of Trey's past abuse resurfaced in her mind. His hateful slurs and cold black eyes invaded her memory. She pressed against the hardwood and lifted her body, not willing to be a punching bag again.

The attacker grabbed her hair and pulled her head backward. She couldn't see him, but his hot breath brushed against her cheek. "Once they find out about you, I'll be back to finish this."

He struck the back of her head and dropped her weakened body to the ground. The gun, still under the dresser, was close. She stretched out her fingers. An inch shy. She tried to scoot closer, but searing pain pierced her body. She couldn't move. Or even stay awake. With one more try, everything faded to black.

Homicide Detective Oz Kelly led the tactical team up the apartment complex stairs and moved with precision down the third-floor corridor. The call of shots fired came in during his shift, and he was the first one at the scene. He stepped around a bag of groceries left behind in the hallway and paused at the entrance until the entire team was in place. Everything seemed quiet except the neighbor's blaring television.

"Mills Creek PD." Oz gave the signal, and the team filed into the room behind him, fanning out across the space. He moved forward, spotted a body on the floor and Liz Burke, one of the department's narcotic's detectives, seated against the living room wall. She held a small brown dog in her lap and an ice pack against her head. Blood streaked her cheek, matted her hair and framed the purple bruises around her right eye.

She looked up at him when he entered. "I was supposed to protect her, not get her killed."

He stepped past the couch and assessed the victim. A young woman who couldn't be more than twenty years old, dark hair with two gunshot wounds—one to the chest and the other to the head. Both fatal.

Oz put away his weapon, crossed to Liz and knelt by her side while other officers secured the scene. He'd seen the newest member of the narcotics team around the precinct, but since they were in different departments, neither had talked much to each other, aside from a polite hello when passing in the hall or break room. She'd already made quite the name for herself as an excellent detective and completed several drug busts since she'd arrived two years ago.

Some of the other officers had been quick to flirt with the pretty new girl, but not him. He had no interest in dating anyone since he'd lost his wife—the only woman he ever loved.

"I'm not sure we've officially met, but I'm Detective Oz Kelly with Homicide."

She took his hand—cold from the ice pack. "Liz Burke, Narcotics."

He helped her to her feet. "Let's move over here so when our medical examiner arrives, she can take care of our victim."

"Thanks." Liz crossed the room and leaned against the kitchen island.

"Who is she?"

"One of my informants."

"And this is her place?"

Liz pulled out a stool and took a seat, the brown dog still in her other arm. "Yeah."

"What were the two of you meeting about?"

She placed the ice pack on the countertop and poked her finger into the squishy plastic. "I can't remember. For the last five minutes, since I came to, I've been trying to recall what happened, but nothing comes to mind."

He motioned to one of the other officers. "Is the ambulance here yet?"

"Just arrived, sir."

He took the dog from Liz's grasp and handed the pet to another investigator. "Let's get you to a hospital so a trauma doc can take a look at the deep gash on your head. Make sure you don't have a brain bleed that could be affecting your memory."

"I'm fine."

"You're not fine if you can't give me a statement on what happened, Detective. Besides, protocol requires you to get checked out." Oz pulled on a pair of gloves and reached for a gunshot residue kit. "Hold out your hands." He dabbed her palms and fingers, then secured the samples for review. "I'll get one of the investigators to run this here. Shouldn't take too long to clear you of firing your weapon."

"I didn't shoot her."

"I never said you did." He held open an evidence bag. "I'll need your gun too." He nodded toward her police-issued weapon in her holster. "Just until you're cleared."

She dropped her weapon inside and zipped the bag closed. "I woke up in the bedroom, and my gun was underneath the dresser. Not sure how it got there, but I'm guessing it was knocked from my hands. What else does the Mills Creek Police protocol require? Will they do an investigation and put me on desk duty?"

"Sounds like you've been through this before."

"Firing a weapon is not an uncommon thing for a former Charlotte narcotics detective."

"You're not in Charlotte anymore, but there was definitely a third party involved." Oz motioned toward Tillie. "There's no bruises on her body, and you look like you've been hit by a truck."

"Flattery will get you nowhere."

He continued, "My guess—the intruder forced his way into the room, shot Tillie and was on his way out when you arrived. You put up a fight and lost." Oz motioned toward the unlatched patio door leading onto a small balcony. "He exited and used the built-in fire escape ladder to descend into the alley below."

"Plausible."

"Clearing you shouldn't be an issue once they collect the evidence if my theory holds up. But first you have to let the paramedic take a look at you."

"Really, I'm okay."

"Tell that to your head." He pointed at her cut, then motioned toward the door. "The guys have told me all about you, so if we could just put the tough act to the side for a moment and get you stitched up then we can check off all the protocol boxes and I won't get reemed out by the sergeant for not following policy."

She stepped into the hallway. "What do you mean they told you about me?"

"You have a reputation around the precinct for being tough and a bit stubborn."

"I do?"

"Let's just say, if this intruder wasn't well trained, they'd be the one with the bruises and potential concussion. Not you."

Her shoulders lifted a bit with the news, and he escorted her down the steps, through the lobby and out the exit door. Cold night air blasted Oz's face with an arctic chill. For three seasons out of the year, he loved living in the Smoky Mountains, but every winter he considered moving to Florida.

Liz shivered next to him, and he motioned for the paramedics to open the ambulance doors so he could get her inside. Once seated on a stretcher, they began their assessment, and Oz stepped back to give her some privacy.

"Wait," she said. "Make sure they're thorough with Tillie. She was my responsibility, and I don't want any evidence overlooked."

He nodded and scanned the growing crowd drawn to the otherwise dark road by police lights and a bustle of activity. Probably just curious onlookers and local journalists hungry for a late-night story. The medical examiner's car pulled to the front of the building. She parked on the street and headed inside.

"Our ME just arrived and is one of the best in the state. Don't worry, we'll figure out what happened. You keep trying to remember the details. We're going to find out who did this to Tillie. I'll check on you later."

Oz closed the doors and headed back upstairs to the crime scene. The apartment was a two bedroom with vaulted ceilings. In the living area, floor-to-ceiling windows rose well above his head. He stepped through the unlocked patio door onto a small balcony and instructed one of the investigators to make sure to dust for prints on the ladder and balcony railing. Not a bad way to flee the scene of a crime without being noticed, but if Liz was unconscious, why not just go back out the front door?

Someone could've parked in the alley below and waited for him to exit. That would minimize exposure to any cameras or nosy neighbors after the shots were fired. Oz looked over the edge. No security cameras. They'd have to canvas every tenant in the building to see if anyone saw anything. He'd make sure to check with the other businesses nearby. Maybe they had security feeds that would give him a glimpse of the intruder or his getaway car.

When he stepped back inside, the medical examiner zipped open the black body bag. Oz shivered at the sound, triggering devastating memories of the night his wife died. Roni had been removed from his home in the same manner—sealed in a body bag and hauled off to a cold dark metal vault to await an autopsy. With every homicide case, he relived the nightmare and vowed justice for this victim's family, no matter who was guilty.

Several hours passed and the only text Oz received from Liz since she'd gone to the hospital, was about Mocha, Tillie's dog. Liz wanted to make sure they found a safe place for the pet to stay. He was impressed. If he'd taken a beating like she had, the last thing on his mind would've been the dog. The thought reminded him of his wife. She'd loved animals too and often took in every stray off the street, hating to see them hungry and cold. Probably why she always persuaded him to help his younger brother, but he'd learned the hard way how enabling a drug addict could ruin one's life.

Oz walked back into Tillie's bedroom. Broken glass from a lamp littered the floor, and a chair was overturned with bloodstains on the side. The investigators had taken photos and bagged a sample of the fabric to test. If the killer was already in CODIS, they'd be able to match his DNA found at a crime scene and identify Tillie's killer. But if the blood was Liz's, then tracking their murderer down would be harder.

"Detective? We thought you might want to look at this." A young female investigator held up a baggie with a pink cell phone inside. "We found it on the kitchen island."

"Thanks. That's helpful. I don't suppose you have her pass code, do you?"

"No, but can't you use her finger? It might be cold but—"

"Won't work. Phone sensors check for the electrical charge running through our bodies. Since she's dead, she's got no charge, and her print alone won't open the device."

The girl shrugged. "I guess you'll have to give it to our cybersecurity team to crack."

Oz had a better idea. Liz was close with the victim, and this looked like a personal phone. Maybe she'd know the pass code. "Thanks. I'll keep that in mind. Other than that, is there any other evidence that might give us a lead on our intruder?"

The girl removed her camera from the bag and scrolled through the screens. "We lifted a couple of shoe prints that don't match Detective Burke or our victim. Probably from the killer. We'll get the size and hopefully the brand when we get back to the lab."

Not exactly a smoking gun, but the info could help them narrow the field of suspects once they had a list.

Another photo of Tillie's hand popped up on the screen. A sapphire and diamond ring sat on her right hand.

"Hold up." He leaned closer. "Can you zoom in on her jewelry?"

The woman clicked a button under her thumb and increased the size of the image. "The piece must've cost a small fortune. If it's real."

"And for a recovering drug addict, I doubt she could afford such a luxury item. Can you send that image to my phone?"

"Sure."

Oz pulled up the latest message from Liz and texted her.

How's it going?

Bored

Do you know Tillie's pin to her personal phone?

0423...her birthday. Told her to change it but doubt she did.

Oz entered the code, and the screen came to life. He scrolled through Tillie's recent call list. He noticed an incoming call not long before her murder that lasted five minutes and seven seconds. Too long for someone she didn't know. The body bag's zipper clicked again—nails on a chalkboard.

"I'm taking her back to the morgue," the medical examiner said.

"Any idea how long the report will take?"

"A few days or a week at the most. Believe it or not, we're somewhat caught up at the moment. Of course, that can change in an instant."

The woman wheeled the stretcher from the room with help from one of her assistants. At least Oz didn't have to look at the black body bag anymore. He took a seat out of the way of the investigation team and continued to peruse Tillie's phone.

"What's going on?" a man's voice echoed into the space. The visitor, approximately five foot ten, one-hundred and fifty pounds, dressed in khaki pants, a sweater vest and ball cap, started to duck under the tape when Oz stood and held up his hand. "Authorized officers only."

The man paused.

"Do you live here?" Oz asked.

"I own the building, and one of my residents called me." He extended a hand. "I'm Joe."

Oz noted the man's wet slicked back hair. Like he'd just stepped out of the shower, threw on some clothes and showed up. Maybe he could provide some insight into the building's security and the residents who lived here.

"I'm Detective Kelly." Oz flashed Tillie's postmortem photo for Joe to view. "Were you two friends?"

The man's face scrunched in disgust. "We talked when we ran into each other but I'm not sure I'd say we were friends. She's only been renting from me for about six months so I hadn't gotten to know her like some of the other tenants. What happened?"

He wasn't going to discuss the details of the case before he notified Tillie's loved ones. Instead, Oz glanced into the hallway. "Do you have security cameras in or around the building?"

"At the elevators. We also have outside cameras at all the entrances and in the parking lot."

"What about the alleyway out back?" Oz ducked underneath the yellow tape.

"I've got one that's a little hidden but still lets us keep an eye on the street."

"Great. Let's go."

Joe led him down the stairwell to the basement floor. The corridor was dark and musty with several metal doors along the left side labeled as supply closets. Dim light filtered through two small windows located at the end. They stopped and Joe unlocked the fourth door, entering into a room with three computer monitors located on a back wall. Oz took a seat and waited for Joe to display the corresponding time stamp.

"Let's play it from there." Oz leaned forward when Liz left the apartment building and headed in the direction of the corner market. That explains the ice cream and pizzas he found in the hallway.

Movement from the corner of the screen caught his attention. Oz looked at the other monitor for a better angle of the area. A large man emerged from a navy blue sedan, but the license plates were not visible. He wore a ball cap with the brim pulled down over his eyes. A dark colored bandanna covered the rest of his face.

Oz pointed to a tattoo on the man's left forearm.

"Zoom in on that." The image pixelated for a moment but then cleared. "That's not good."

Joe looked at him. "What's it mean?"

"Make a copy for me, please." He handed the man a USB drive instead of answering his question, wanting to keep the details of the case confidential.

Oz had seen the markings before. Military. Special Forces. The kind of turncoat killer trained in stealth attacks, assault missions and marksmanship. Once discharged from the army, a few struggled to find their place in the world again and joined private security teams to regain a sense of purpose, but when they worked for the wrong company, mountains of money turned trained soldiers into mercenaries who hunted their targets until the mission was complete. If Liz was next on the list, then her life was in grave danger.

TWO

Four hours later and too many tests that ruled out a brain bleed, Liz took a car service back to the crime scene. The doctor diagnosed her with a concussion and traumatic amnesia, a condition that sometimes occurs after a head injury. According to his information and one scary internet search, she might not ever be able to remember the attack details, but he recommended plenty of rest and a sabbatical from work. That was never going to happen, not if she had anything to say about it. The man who shot Tillie was still out there, and a few days of rest wasn't going to help her find him.

Liz knocked back a couple of ibuprofen, washed them down with a free bottled water and stepped out of the car, paying the nice driver his fee.

A few snow flurries melted on her face, and cold wind chilled her to the bone. She didn't look forward to reentering the crime scene, but now that she was cleared and alert, she wanted another look.

With a tug on the building door, she stepped into the lobby, trying to remember anything about her visit with Tillie. Her boot heels clacked against the marble tile and the scent of evening coffee wafted in her direction. She noted the elevators and their security cameras nearby, making a mental note to check the footage.

Liz took a left and climbed the same stairwell as earlier. She'd been talking to Aggie when she took these steps. That she remembered. Maybe her cousin would be able to tell her about the moment. A bag of groceries sat at the edge of the hallway. Liz crouched down and peered inside. Melted chocolate ice cream oozed from the edge of the container and covered two thawed pizzas and one can of dog food. She lifted the bag and tossed the items into the trash, then made her way to Tillie's apartment.

Before she entered, the neighbor's door opened. Mocha barked at Liz from the woman's arms.

"I hope it's okay. I told the officer I'd keep Tillie's dog until a more permanent home can be found. I've got plenty of food for the pup, and my poodle loves having a new buddy."

"Thank you so much, Mrs....?"

"Jenner. Carol Jenner."

"Did you see what happened here? Did anyone unusual enter Tillie's apartment earlier this evening?"

"Well, you, of course. And a man. He was tall like my George, God rest his soul."

Liz took out a notepad and pen. "Did you get a look at his face?"

"Only saw the back of his dark head, but he got into a navy blue sedan when he left."

She jotted the information down. Maybe they could track the car and get the registration. "What about the license plate tag?"

The woman shook her head and ran her fingers through Mocha's fur. "I'm sorry. That's all I saw."

"Did you hear any gunshots?"

The woman straightened. "I did hear a couple of pops. About fifteen minutes after I heard you close the door. I looked out my window because I thought the sound came from the street, but my hearing isn't as good as it used to be when I was young like you. That's when I saw the car."

"Anything else?"

"'Fraid not. Except for this little cutie barking." The older woman scratched the dog's head.

Liz pulled a card from her pocket. "If you think of something, give me a call."

"Of course."

She gave Mocha a pat, said her goodbyes and then signed the crime scene log to enter Tillie's apartment. A few investigators still milled about the room, gathering their tools while crime scene cleaners removed the bloodstains from the hardwood floors.

Oz scrolled through digital images on Tillie's personal phone, the pink one she'd left on the kitchen island. He looked up when she entered. "That was fast. I figured they'd keep you overnight for observation."

"They wanted to, but I talked the doc into letting me rest at home. Once my head scan was cleared, he agreed and discharged me. I've got a concussion and I'm sure a large bill coming."

"But you're supposed to be home, resting?"

Liz folded her arms. "Work is restful for me. Besides, I was losing my mind not knowing the status of our case. Anything on our killer's ID?"

"Not yet. We took blood samples and sent them to the lab, but it will be a while before we get a report."

Oz motioned toward the door. "There's a sitting area

near the elevators. Let's go out there and let these guys finish up."

She followed him to the alcove and plopped onto the small couch beside him.

"How are you feeling? Do you remember what happened?"

"Still nothing." She leaned back, inhaling the faded spiced scent of cologne as he slipped on his blazer. "If I could just make the pain go away a little faster, then maybe I could be of more help."

"What about before you were hit? Do you remember driving here?"

She squinted an eye at him, the overhead light intensifying the pain. "The only thing I remember is going to the store, buying dog food and talking to my cousin. Everything else is a blank. I can't remember what Tillie and I discussed before I left or who attacked me."

Oz retrieved his cell phone from his pocket and handed it to her, then tapped the play key. "Maybe this will help."

Liz leaned forward and watched the video, ignoring her head's constant throb. "Is this the only camera angle we have?"

"This is the one outside, and we have one at the elevator, but I didn't see you or him on that footage."

"I'm not big on tight spaces that move. I took the stairs. He probably did too. Is this our guy?"

"Yeah. He had a getaway car waiting in the alley. Anything about him look familiar?"

"You mean the top of his ball cap? Nope." She paced to the window and looked down at the short side street. Trauma had a funny way of affecting people. She couldn't remember anything about her current attack but the past abuse she'd endured never seemed to fade. What she wouldn't give to erase every hit that still haunted her after two years. "The neighbor said she saw him get into a navy blue sedan."

"Can she ID him?"

"Only the back of his head getting into the car."

"That's okay. We're running his tattoo through the database."

Liz looked at the phone again. "Military?"

"Probably former Special Forces. Trained and lethal."

"Great." She handed his cell back to him. "That's more than a tattoo. That's a death sentence. You and I both know he'll come back until all witnesses are eliminated. I'm just surprised he let me live."

"Yeah. Me too." Oz stood. "Let's head back to the precinct. I can take your statement, give Tillie's phone to the cybersecurity team and line up a safe house for you tonight. Some rest will help your memory, then we can figure out who he is and if he's coming back for you."

She followed Oz into the stairwell. "I don't want to be hidden away. I want to find this guy and I can't do that in some police safe house."

"You know the drill. We have to follow protocol. You're the only eyewitness and that alone requires protection." Oz tapped out a message to their captain while they descended the stairs. "Maybe something in one of your case files with Tillie will help us uncover who's behind this, then we might be able to keep the assassin he hired from killing you."

"Finding the moneyman is a long shot and you know it. The cartels are really good at keeping all their minions in the dark."

"Then we follow the chain from Tillie up. Has to

lead somewhere." He flipped his screen for her to read. "Safe house is set up. Captain's orders."

"Great." The idea of sleeping in some dingy room with a detective she barely knew creeped her out. Oz seemed nice enough, but Trey had been nice in the beginning too. Plus, she wanted to sleep in a comfortable bed, not some hard twin mattress that hadn't been cleaned in months.

She stopped at the exit door of the building. "How about this? My father has a cabin on Lake Marie. He was former military before he retired and moved to Florida. The place is off-grid with its own power supply, and a full security system, better than anything we have in one of our safe houses. Very few neighbors live there and close up their places for the winter. No one will find me."

Another ache shot across her forehead, and she leaned against the door frame as a wave of nausea swept through her body.

Oz placed a hand on her arm. "Are you okay?"

The cool metal felt good on her cheek. "I will be if I'm allowed to stay at the lake cabin. I need to be somewhere I'm comfortable…to help me remember."

"Our policy is for you to be guarded twenty-four seven when under a protective order, and you can't be alone. Especially not with your injury and an assassin on the loose. I'll go with you."

He reminded Liz of her former partner—the type of cop who always followed the rules to the letter of the law, leaving little room for instinct and common sense. Not that she didn't obey orders, but sometimes detectives had to make tough calls and trust their gut. "That's not necessary. I'm a trained cop. Out of the Charlotte precinct. I've taken on some of the area's worst drug cartels and can handle a lone assassin."

"And you had a team of officers helping you."

The nausea eased and she straightened. "I'll be fine."

"You don't even have a weapon anymore."

"My dad stocks a secret panic room with a cache of weapons, including rocket launchers and hand grenades. He taught me how to use them all. Besides, if anyone comes nosing around, I'll lock myself inside the panic room or escape through the underground tunnel. The United States Army won't even be able to get me out."

"They don't have to get you out. They just have to get in." Oz folded his arms across his chest. "Let me come with you so I can fulfill my orders and we can work the case together. That's the only way we end this."

He made a good point. "Fine, but only because I can't drive with a concussion."

Liz pressed open the exterior door and walked to Oz's unmarked SUV, then slid into the passenger seat. Her whole body ached. Maybe having Oz along wouldn't be so bad.

His overprotective nature alarmed her a bit even though Oz's concern seemed genuine. After Trey, she questioned every act of kindness or offer of support. The bruises had healed, but he'd left behind nasty scars of skepticism. Was Oz a man she could trust? They were colleagues, and he seemed legit, but she'd thought that about Trey too. Some of her best friends turned their back on her and vanished after their breakup even though most of them witnessed her bruises and knew what kind of man he was.

"I want to take another look at the evidence the team

collected from the crime scene. Mind if we make a stop at the precinct?"

"Sure." She settled in her seat, closed her eyes and tried to walk back through what she could remember about the attack. She remembered Tillie's initial call, how scared the girl was, also walking to the store and having a conversation with her cousin, but nothing after that.

Her head nodded to the side and Liz opened her eyes. "That was fast."

Oz pulled into a parking space at the police parking lot. "You dozed off. Maybe that doctor was right about needing rest."

She did feel a bit better after her power nap. She exited the car, then followed Oz into the building. They headed toward the large evidence room and signed in at the desk. Oz pulled a couple of boxes from the shelves and placed them on a middle table. Fluorescent lights buzzed overhead, and dust, floating in the glow, tempted her to sneeze. Instead, Liz donned a pair of gloves, removed the lid and peered inside at Tillie's personal items.

She pushed a bottle of perfume and a jewelry box dotted with blood to the side while pulling several photos from the bottom. After flipping through them, she settled on one.

A handsome dark-haired man draped his arm around Tillie's shoulders. Her informant gazed up at him with a genuine smile etched on her face.

"Who's this?" Liz held out the photo for Oz to view. The man looked familiar, but she couldn't quite place him.

Oz leaned in for a closer look. "That's Judd Thoreau. He's her father's business partner."

"He makes her happy."

"Looks that way."

"Don't you find that odd? Her staring up at this man who's at least twice her age with a goofy look on her face. Looks like she loves him." Liz flipped the photo over. "This wasn't that long ago. You don't think there was something going on between them, do you?"

"I wouldn't think so since he works with her father, but then again—" he took another look at the picture "—who knows these days."

Liz placed the image under a lighted magnifier and scoured every corner for details. Fall decorations enhanced the background. Corn husks and carved pumpkins sat on the side of a rock fireplace. "This looks like a party at someone's very nice house."

"Probably her father's home. They hold a large fall festival and invite all their wealthy friends to their estate in West Park Hills. He knows some powerful people and this party helps raise funds for their campaigns or charities."

"Tillie never mentioned that to me. In fact, she told me her father lived on the West Coast."

"Then she lied to you."

"But why? She trusted me and always gave good information. Why would she lie about her father? Seems unlikely."

"Yeah, right." He shot her a disbelieving look. "We ask our informants to lie and betray people they once called friends to gain information for our cases. None of them are trustworthy."

"True, and it wouldn't be the first time a recovering addict hasn't been truthful, but I thought Tillie was different." She returned the photos to the box. "She didn't have a motive to lie. Being honest benefited her."

"That doesn't mean she told you the truth about everything." He returned his box to the shelf. "Both her parents live in town. Have for years. Looks like Tillie left out a few details when she found out you weren't from Mills Creek."

"Both her parents?"

"Her mom and dad. They're still married as far as I know."

The young woman Liz had worked so hard to protect had deceived her. Not that she expected her to be honest about everything, but why would she lie about her parents? Tillie acted like she truly wanted to change her life, but if she was willing to lie about her family, then what else had she hidden?

"She told me her name was Tillie Blue. Even had a driver's license to back up her story. Does that match up?"

"Along with several other aliases we found in Tillie's drawers. She had plenty of identities. But if you don't believe me, then here's a family photo forwarded from her phone." He pulled up the image. "Do you recognize him?"

Liz leaned against the table, stunned by the man in the picture. "Is that Jeremiah Foxx?"

"The CEO of the largest financial investment firm in the southeast and Tillie's father. Wouldn't surprise me if her death had something to do with one of his business deals gone wrong. We need to look back at cases connected to her father. He's known around town to have several enemies."

"Sounds like a good way to pass the time at the lake house."

"And we might be able to trigger your memory in

the process while figuring out a solid theory for why someone would want her dead."

She hated to think Tillie's father had anything to do with his daughter's death but the idea gave Liz some much-needed relief from the guilt she'd been carrying. Since waking up and finding her young informant on the floor, she'd blamed herself. If only she'd never pulled Tillie into their undercover drug operations, then her friend might still be alive. Liz wanted to sort through all the evidence until they found Tillie's killer, then she'd make him pay.

They stepped outside and Liz pulled her coat collar higher to block the cold wind. The one thing she missed about Charlotte was the warmer weather, and despite her fondness of a pretty snow, she wasn't much for the frigid mountain temperatures.

Small businesses along Main Street had closed up for the night, eliminating any traffic. Snow flurries continued to float through the air, dusting park benches and sidewalks in white powder.

They were the only two people outside, as if the whole town was theirs.

Liz reached his parked SUV, spotlighted by the glow of a streetlamp, and Oz opened the door for her. Another thoughtful gesture by him without any hesitation. Maybe Oz was different from Trey.

Before she climbed into the warm cabin, she glanced up the hill. All the spaces were empty except for one—with a navy blue sedan.

Oz ran around the front of the SUV and slid inside, cranking the engine to life. "Hold on."

Liz clutched the door handle during his sharp U-turn,

but he didn't slow down. He couldn't or their suspect might get away.

The navy blue sedan veered down a side street. Oz followed, flipped on his lights and siren, then called for backup.

"Do you think they came back for me?" Liz pressed the seat belt into place.

"Perhaps." He steered right, down a dark street. Red taillights traversed a hill at least five hundred feet away. He stepped on the gas, launching them airborne for a second as they bounced through a dip. "Sometimes criminals return to the scenes of their crimes."

"Not professionals. They move on to the next job." She adjusted the shoulder strap. "Which means I am the *next job.*"

Oz took another side road, hoping to cut the car off. If he could just gain some distance, he might catch him. "Do you see the car?"

"Nothing."

He gripped the steering wheel tighter and scanned the area, slowing his speed to make sure he didn't miss anything. Either the driver knew another way out of the area or he'd pulled into a hiding spot.

"I think we've lost them," Liz said.

"I'll have Dispatch put out a BOLO. Maybe one of the patrol officers will come across the car."

He turned his vehicle in the opposite direction and glanced at the clock. Midnight. "It's late but I still need to inform Tillie's family about her death. I don't want them hearing the news from the press."

Liz flipped down the passenger-side mirror and ran her fingers through her dark hair. "I'd rather not let them see me like this. I'm gross."

He started to argue but stopped himself. She was his colleague. His very attractive colleague, and complimenting her looks would be crossing a line. "Probably best if I talk to them alone anyway. If they find out she was working with you, then there will be a whole host of questions we're not ready to answer."

"Agreed. I'll wait in the car."

He pulled into the circular drive, made his way to the entrance of the luxury estate and delivered the devastating news. The family was sad but not shocked.

"We're not surprised, Detective." Jeremiah Foxx, Tillie's father, loomed in the doorway, not inviting Oz inside. "Our daughter chose friends who always got her in trouble and although we are saddened by this turn of events, we've expected a knock on our door for years."

Turn of events? The man sounded like he was talking about a failed business deal instead of his daughter's murder. "Do you know any of these friends she hung out with?"

Mr. Foxx turned to his wife, who stood quietly beside him. "What was that kid's name she was with the day she left?"

Miranda Foxx wiped a tear from her cheek. "Milton something. I don't remember his last name."

"Do you know where we can find him?"

She shook her head and turned away from the door, disappearing into the interior of the home.

"Please excuse my wife. She's always maintained an unrealistic hope that Tillie would come back. I tried to prepare her for this day but she kept believing our daughter would change. A mother's heart I suppose never gives up but I knew different."

"If you think of anything else, please give me a call."

Oz handed him a card, then excused himself and returned to the SUV.

"How'd they take it?" Liz asked when he climbed back inside.

"Surprisingly well. It was odd. That's the part of the job I usually hate but he made her death seem uneventful."

"That *is* odd. Although people do grieve in many different ways. Maybe he's in a bit of denial and the emotions will hit him later."

"Let's hope so. Otherwise, the man's a robot."

Oz pulled away from the three-story home, surrounded by lush gardens and a well-lit fountain spraying water into the air. A hazy fog surrounded the five-acre property. Seemed appropriate regarding the news he'd just delivered. Not even a large home in a prime area of town protected a father from his worst nightmare—losing a daughter. Death came to all eventually—the great equalizer.

"What about her mom? Isn't her name Miranda?"

Oz nodded and turned onto the main road. "She shed a few tears, then went back inside. That's when he told me his wife had always hoped Tillie would come back home but he knew it would never happen."

Liz straightened. "She was planning to return home after she got a bit more stable on her own. She wanted to reconcile with them. Why would he say something like that? He couldn't know whether she'd return or not?"

"Unless he's the one who had her killed. He certainly has the money to hire a hitman."

"But his own daughter? That's so heartless."

"Unfortunately. I've seen worse."

Liz's phone buzzed with a message, but she flipped

over the screen without even a glance. She caught him staring. "It's not important."

"I wasn't gonna ask. Your phone, your business."

She shoved the device into her bag's side pocket then shifted away from him, but not before he noticed a flash of worry on her face.

"Hey—" he reached over and touched her arm "—you okay?"

"Yeah. Fine."

Whatever had her concerned remained locked away in the recesses of her mind. He was fine if she wasn't ready to discuss the issue with him but something had happened while he was inside the Foxx's residence and he hoped she wasn't keeping pertinent evidence to herself.

The snowfall intensified and he turned up his wipers to help him see the road. "This snow is heavy."

She didn't respond. He tried again.

"Do you need me to stop at your place to pick up some clothes?"

Liz still didn't answer. He weaved toward the edge of the road and back.

Her hand grabbed for the dash. "What was that? Did you almost hit something?"

"Sorry. My bad."

Back to silence.

"I thought we could swing by your place and pick up an overnight bag for you."

"Sounds good," Liz said and returned her gaze back to the window. Maybe the text was none of his business but whatever or whoever messaged her had Liz completely distracted. They both needed a good night's sleep, and then he'd broach the subject again, tomorrow.

Oz made a quick stop at her apartment for her things before getting back on the main interstate. They still had an hour's drive before arriving at Lake Marie, and he wasn't sure he could keep his eyes open that long.

"We're not far from my house. Mind if we stay there tonight, then head to your dad's lake cabin tomorrow? I'm exhausted and don't think I can make the long drive this late. And before you ask, yes, I have a guest room."

"I'm pretty beat too, but do you think we'll be safe there?"

"I've got a top-of-the-line security system, a gun safe with weapons and I've been keeping an eye out for any tails. So far, we're clear."

"Then I guess we're staying at your house."

Oz took the next interstate exit and turned right, thankful that she'd agreed. He couldn't wait to crash in his own bed.

"You know, I've been asking about you around the department." She glanced in his direction.

"Really?" His gut knotted. The last five years, some of his colleagues had seen him at his worst. He hoped they hadn't shared any of those moments. "Why?"

"When I started this narcotics job, I reviewed some past cases to get a feel for the environment. The dynamic is pretty different from the Charlotte PD, but both areas have similar issues. Anyway, I came across a couple of your cases. You did a lot of good work and made my job easier because of your arrest record. You shut down some serious operations in the area."

"Our team worked hard, and the results are not mine alone." He paused. "So, what did my colleagues say?"

"They gave me a bit more info. Said you're one of the best detectives they know."

The panic coursing through him eased a bit. "That's cool."

"And you would give a person the shirt off your back if they needed it."

He'd helped several of them when they were going through difficult times. His late wife had often opened up his eyes to recognize when someone was struggling. She was the one who drove his generosity with her kind-hearted nature. The same sweet naivety that got her killed.

"My team's been through a lot of challenges together over the years and we help each other during the most devastating moments of our lives. They did the same for me when Roni died."

Liz reached for the knob and turned down the slow southern rock song playing on the radio. "They mentioned her death. Said she died at home the night you busted up one of the largest drug rings in the area. Must have been quite the tragedy."

Memories of Roni on the floor, blood all around her, flashed through his mind. He would never be able to erase the last time he saw her. The vivid image haunted him. "I don't like to talk about it."

She paused. "We all have a past. I'm not looking for details. I thought you could help me with a way to move on from the guilt of failing someone you promised to protect. How did you cope?"

He tapped the turn signal and let the rhythmic ticking give him time to gather his words. The gory details of his wife's death still plagued him even though five years had passed. The local and national news camped out on his lawn for months, hoping for a statement from the grieving husband. Some internet trolls even accused him of the murder until the police department made a statement about his ironclad alibi.

Reporters followed him to and from work, calling him on the phone and asking him all kinds of questions. Even to this day, many still wanted to know if he talked to the man convicted of the crime. His answer was always a resounding no. He didn't talk to his younger brother anymore or discuss his gory testimony of how the strung-out monster killed his wife.

"I didn't. The guilt still plagues me to this day, but somehow, by the grace of God, I suppose, you keep moving forward."

Familiar pain reflected in her eyes. "I left Tillie alone. Only for a few minutes, but I knew better. Assassins track their prey and wait for an opportunity to strike. She'd still be alive if I'd stayed."

"Or you'd both be dead."

Liz tugged at a long strand of dark hair draped across her shoulder. "She told me weeks ago she was receiving threats. I should've called witness protection then."

"You can always play the what-if game, but the outcome never changes. Your victim is still dead, and a killer is still out there. There's not a day that goes by that I don't wonder if Roni would still be here if I'd been home that night or if I'd never let my brother, Clay, back into our lives, but at some point you have to stop blaming yourself and put the responsibility on the one who pulled the trigger."

"If only I could remember who that was."

"Give it time."

She paused for a moment, then looked at him again. "Your brother killed your wife?"

Oz tightened his grip on the steering wheel, not meaning to open *that* conversation. Most people in town didn't bring the topic up anymore. They understood the deep pain his brother had caused, Oz's decline into alcoholism and the strength of God that pulled him back to living a full life. Those who knew him never wanted to remind him of those dark days, but Liz hadn't lived in town then. Of course, she had questions about his wife's homicide and his brother's conviction.

"He did."

"If you don't mind my asking, what happened?"

"My brother was addicted to drugs and had been to rehab several times but never was able to beat his addiction. He'd do anything for a hit. The day my wife was killed, he called asking me for money. Even made up some excuse about a friend needing gas for a trip, but I knew he was lying and refused to give him anything."

Liz's gaze remained on him, heavy, attentive and listening.

"After I left for work that night, he went to my house and broke in through our back patio door. He knew where I kept a cash stash for emergencies. My wife heard the glass shatter and came downstairs with a bat. When she saw my brother, she picked up her phone and told him she was going to call me. That's when he shot her three times in the chest. She died within a matter of seconds and my brother fled the scene without being caught that night."

"That's awful."

"What's worse is some accused me of killing her. The husband's always the guilty party, right?"

"Only if that's what the evidence reveals."

"Thankfully my colleagues in the Homicide Department collected the evidence and knew my alibi. I suspected my brother as soon as I found the cash missing, but we had to find him to prove he pulled the trigger. My sergeant put me on leave and quoted policy about not working family cases, which I get, but I couldn't sit by and do nothing. I knew I was the only one who could track down Clay. Two days later, I found him hiding in a barn at his dealer's house. He still had the gun on him and I brought him in for questioning. After an hour of interrogation, he confessed."

"Wow. I can't even begin to imagine what that must've been like for you."

"Devastating and not really something I like to discuss when I'm exhausted."

"Of course. I get it. I don't like to talk about my past either."

A couple of cars drove by, their headlights glaring off the wet road. Oz refrained from telling her about his own decline into alcoholism, depression and a plethora of bad decisions after his wife's death. If not for a couple of his friends from church reaching out and convincing him to get help, he wasn't sure where he'd be today.

"I told you mine."

Liz shifted her gaze from his. "Nothing like that, just a bad breakup. So what happened to your brother?"

That was a not-so-subtle deflection if he'd ever seen one, but he decided not to press the issue. She'd talk when she was ready for him to know more. "He's in jail. I testified against him, and the judge sentenced him to twenty-five years in prison without parole."

"You lost two loved ones that night," Liz said. "Must still be hard even now."

Oz turned the radio volume key back up. "I lost my brother long before he killed Roni. His addiction to drugs took the Clay I knew, years ago. Forgiving him is the hardest thing I've ever done. Even harder than grieving the loss of my wife."

Silence settled between them as Oz wound the SUV down the two-lane road into the countryside. Roni had loved the remote area of their home, but he often wondered if they'd lived closer to Mills Creek with nearby neighbors, would his brother have been so bold to break into their home? Would he have made a different decision that night if she hadn't been so isolated in the country? "My place is only another couple of miles ahead."

"Sure is a long way out here."

"Did you live in the city?"

"Close. There was a neighborhood that butted up to the edge of Charlotte, and we fixed up an older house."

"We?"

"Yeah. The bad breakup I mentioned earlier, and one terrible mistake, but that's long over."

"He's not a problem anymore?"

She shifted her gaze again and glanced at the pocket where she'd stowed her phone. "Nothing I can't handle."

He started to ask her more as they rounded a curve into a long straightaway but headlights from an oncoming truck brightened toward them. Despite the distance, the wet roads intensified the glare.

Oz raised a hand and flashed his brights, hoping the driver would dim his, but instead the truck veered into their lane and accelerated.

Liz grabbed the handle above her head. "What's he doing?"

"I have no idea. He must be intoxicated."

Oz pressed the horn. The driver kept coming.

He turned on his siren and blue lights, hoping to alter

the truck's course or make him stop. Usually, the threat of being pulled over scared most drivers, especially those who were driving under the influence of drugs or alcohol, but not this time. Liz grabbed the radio. "Control. This is 3-Adam-15. Send backup to Red School Road. We have a possible 10-55."

Dispatch called all units to the scene with the closest patrol at least five minutes out. Oz slowed their car and steered to the other side of the road but the driver mimicked his moves.

"Is he playing chicken?" Liz asked.

"Looks like it."

The truck came closer.

Faster.

Less than a mile apart.

"He's going to hit us." Liz grabbed for her weapon. "I don't have my gun. Give me yours."

Oz rolled down his window. "Here, you steer. I'll shoot."

She slid across the console, grabbed the wheel and kept their speed under thirty miles per hour.

"Don't stop completely. We might need to steer around him. Especially if he's high or drunk."

"I don't think he's either. His moves are intentional."

Oz unbuckled his seat belt, leaned out the window and aimed at the tires. He fired two rounds. The truck swerved but kept coming.

"Oz…"

He shot again.

"Oz…"

Missed.

"Oz!"

He dropped back inside, grabbed the wheel and

swerved off the road. The truck accelerated past them without stopping.

They bounded down the embankment. Metal crunched and lights bounced off the trees. The SUV rolled several times, and stings of shattered glass pelted his face, drawing blood. Each rotation slammed his body into the driver's-side door or the steering wheel, bruising his torso and head with each hit. Airbags struck his chest and knocked the wind from his lungs. Nature accelerated around them but slowed at the same time, as if motion and gravity battled for control.

A large tree stopped their descent into the darkness. Oz sat still for a moment, dazed from the trauma, and pain reverberated through every muscle in his body.

He had to get Liz out. The truck's aggressive driving wasn't an accident. The driver had found them and forced them to wreck. Another attempt to take out the only witness to Tillie's murder.

Oz reached across the console and touched her arm. Warm and soft but also limp. He pushed against her skin, but weakness flooded through his arm and black shadows invaded his vision. He licked his lips, the metallic taste of blood on them.

Tires squalled in the distance, and distant sirens echoed through the night air. His body refused to respond no matter how much he wanted to help.

Liz.

THREE

The warmth of the car escaped through the broken glass, and a bone-cold chill wrapped around Liz's body, rousing her dazed state. White airbags puffed around her and a constant ring played in her ears, but after moving her arms and legs with little pain, she ruled out any injuries—a blessing of protection after the dangerous crash. Everything happened so fast.

Her fingers trembled as she reached for Oz's hand. "Are you okay?"

He didn't answer nor did he squeeze her fingers back. She looked over at him. Blood dripped down the side of his face, and his eyes were closed. The rise and fall of his chest alleviated any initial fears of serious injury, but his pulse was weak as she pressed two fingers against his neck.

"Oz. Wake up."

She pushed against his shoulder, but the man didn't move. Maybe his injuries were worse than they looked. Liz shifted in her seat, leaned across the console and rubbed her knuckles up and down his sternum. "Come on."

He raised his eyelids and closed them. She pressed again, a bit harder this time. "Stay with me. Wake up."

Oz blinked a couple of times, inhaled and sat up straight. "Liz?"

"I'm here."

"Are you okay?"

"I've got a few more bruises to match the others." She opened the glove box. "Do you have a first-aid kit?"

"Its in the back." He exited the car, moved to the back of the SUV and retrieved an orange trauma bag, then climbed back inside. "Are you hurt?" He unzipped the top. "What do you need?"

"It's for you." She retrieved a couple of alcohol swabs and some butterfly bandages, then reached toward his face. Oz leaned away from her touch.

"Why?"

"There's a cut on your cheek, and it isn't going to stop bleeding by itself."

He pulled down the sun visor and looked into the mirror. "I guess it could've been worse. I removed my seat belt to make the shots. I'm fortunate I wasn't thrown from the car. This is minor compared to what could've happened."

Liz scooted a bit closer, cleaned the injury and applied the bandages. His dark eyes lowered when she looked at him. A red tinge blushed the skin underneath her fingers. They'd never been this close before, but for such a handsome man, she hadn't expected him to be shy around women. With his looks, she figured an endless supply of ladies were available. He seemed nervous around her, and she didn't know whether to be flattered or offended.

Instead of prolonging his obvious discomfort, she pressed the edges of the strips in place, making sure they adhered to his skin, then moved back to her seat.

"That should hold for a while. I don't think it's deep enough for stitches."

"Good to know." Oz retrieved his phone from his back pocket. "No service. What about you?"

She looked at her screen. "Same."

He reached across the console with a slight groan from the movement, lifted the police radio from the holder and called again for backup.

"Make sure to have them send a paramedic too. They need to take a look at you."

"I'm fine."

"Said the man who just groaned while reaching for the radio." Liz bit back a smile at the annoyed look he shot her while relaying the details to Dispatch. All available units were en route to their location. Now all they had to do was wait and try to keep warm.

Oz turned the ignition key. To her surprise, the engine started and heat blew against her face. She held her icy fingers to the vents. "We're heating the woods more than ourselves with all the shattered windows."

"True but at least it will help a little."

"Any thoughts on the truck who almost hit us?"

The whole incident was a blur, but one thing was clear—the driver left no questions about his intentions. He wanted her dead and wouldn't stop even if killing her took out innocent people like Oz. The last thing she needed was another death on her shoulders, but these men meant business. They played to kill or be killed.

Oz zipped up his jacket. "How'd they even know our location?"

"I guess we *did* have a tail."

"But I was so careful."

"Maybe a tracking device of some kind? They could've placed it on the car while we were at Tillie's apartment."

"Her phone." Oz reached into his pocket and pulled out the device. "I was looking through it at the crime scene and meant to turn it in when we were at the precinct but forgot."

"No wonder they were able to track us."

He scrolled through the settings and turned off the location service. "That should help. I'll get one of our team to return it to Evidence. Maybe that will keep us hidden when we get to the safe house."

"You know how assassins work. They've been trained to track people down with their vast network of hired lowlifes willing to do their bidding for a bankroll. The question isn't if they will find us again but when."

"Not if we track them down first." Oz pointed at his dash cam on the windshield and pulled up the corresponding time stamped footage on his laptop still secured on the stand and hit Play.

"Anything? Identifying features? Glimpse of the driver?"

He shook his head. "The lights were too bright."

She stared at the image. The beam glared right into the camera before they swerved. They still had nothing to indicate who might be targeting her.

A sad country song played on the radio, and Oz took her hand in his. "I'm glad you're okay."

She smiled and met his gaze, fully aware of the heat traveling through her entire body at his touch. He was a cop, like her ex, a line she wasn't willing to cross with a colleague again. She pulled her hand away and tried the door, but it was jammed. Probably from the roll. "Not gonna budge."

"You can use mine once backup gets here. If you don't mind crawling across the con—"

"Did you see that?" Liz stared through her side mirror into the darkness behind them. A faint streak of light caught her attention. The beam pointed to the ground.

"What?"

"I thought I saw movement behind us." She slid lower in her seat. "There, a faint glow. Five o'clock. See it?"

Oz's hand pressed her farther toward the floor. "Get down."

A barrage of bullets pummeled the passenger-side door as two men in black hid behind large tree trunks for cover. "How'd they get here so quick?"

"Must've come up a back road." Oz pulled out his weapon and checked to see how many bullets he had left. "I've only got six rounds. We need to move. If we don't get out of the car, then backup is going to find two corpses in the seats when they arrive."

If she crossed the console for Oz's door, they'd hit her for sure. "We're sitting ducks here."

Oz grabbed his handle and shoved his shoulder into the driver's-side door. For a moment, the gunfire paused as their enemies reloaded. Oz stepped out and pulled the back door open too, then grabbed her hand.

"Come on."

Liz stayed as low as she could and slid on her belly into wet leaves outside the SUV. Shots started again. They used the doors for cover, and Oz fired his weapon to keep the assassins at bay.

"These guys don't quit, do they?"

"Don't you have a spare weapon?"

"In the console."

She leaned back across the driver's seat, grabbed the gun and found a good line of sight to return fire.

Distant sirens echoed through the trees, and blue lights lit up the wooded area. The two men fled from their location. No way was she going to let them disappear after almost killing her. She took off after them, moving from tree to tree.

"Liz, don't!"

She glanced back over her shoulder but didn't stop. The two men slid down another embankment as she reached the top and looked over.

A back road at the bottom wound out to the main highway. Red taillights faded again from view, and her assailants were gone. Another missed chance. Liz turned and headed back toward the car just as Oz caught up.

"Have you lost your mind? We're trying to keep you away from the assassins, not have you chase them down."

She walked past him. "Better than being a sitting duck. I didn't become a cop to hide."

He fell into step beside her as they walked back toward the wreckage. "I want them too, but we have to be smart about our moves, and chasing two snipers into the woods without backup isn't protocol."

"Sometimes you have to go with your gut, and that's what I did."

"Going with your gut is what gets people killed. That's not the way we do things at Mills Creek."

No matter what response she gave, nothing was going to change the determined look on Oz's face. She was the newest member of the team, and despite having a stellar record in her former job, she hadn't proven her skills with her colleagues yet. They didn't trust her and neither did Oz.

A bright light spotlighted them from above and their rescuers descended down to them, assessing the damage.

Oz's partner, Detective Bronson Young, reached them first. "Good to see you both alive. From the looks of your truck, I wasn't sure what I was going to find."

"Thankfully, our injuries are minor." Oz shook his partner's hand. "Thanks for the entry. Probably kept us from getting shot."

"However, Oz may have broken some ribs from the roll. Can we get a paramedic to check him out?" Liz shook Bronson's hand too.

"I've had broken ribs before, and mine are fine."

"Not according to the groan in the car, and didn't you just tell me we need to follow protocol? That's all I'm doing, right, Bronson?"

His partner held up his hands in surrender. "I'm with her, buddy. Won't hurt to get them looked at."

"*Now* you want to follow protocol." Oz shot her an annoyed look, then turned his attention back to his friend. "Let's head back up."

Bronson flashed his light to the ground. "I've got paramedics at the top, and they can check you both out." He picked up a bullet casing and held it up for them to see. "How many shots did they fire at you two?"

"At least twenty rounds. Maybe more." Liz walked to the passenger's side of the totaled SUV. "After we wrecked, our attackers parked on a back road about five hundred feet down that embankment, climbed the hill and opened fire from that tree."

"Did you get a good look at them?"

"Not really. They wore camouflage paint on their

faces, and when they came at us on the road, they had their lights on bright," Liz said.

"We may have a lead on the truck. One of our patrol officers radioed with traffic cam footage of a large truck with spotlights speeding through an intersection at Peachtree and Madison." Bronson held out a hand to her and helped both of them climb over a fallen tree. "The time stamp coincides with your dispatch call and the shooting."

"Any idea who the vehicle is registered to?" Liz asked.

"Not specifically," Bronson huffed as he climbed the steepest part of the hill. "We traced the rental back to a large fleet company. Anyone could've scheduled the truck online and then used the vehicle to run y'all off the road. I'm going to send investigators to the local branch in the morning and see if they can provide a list of customers."

Oz stopped near Bronson's car at the top of the hill. "Can we get their surveillance footage while you're there? Maybe we can identify the person who picked the car up."

"I'll try, but they don't like to give out customer or company names without a search warrant." Bronson held out his keys. "Take my SUV. I'll get one of the others to drop me back at the precinct."

"Thanks, man." Oz gave him a fist bump. "One more thing." He handed his partner Tillie's pink phone. "Will you give this to the cyber team? See if there's anything on it that will give us a lead?"

"Absolutely."

Liz slid into the passenger seat, every muscle in her body tense. They were still at square one in their case and tonight, she'd almost gotten Oz killed too. One thing she did know—this murderer was determined to keep her from talking, and they wouldn't stop until she was silenced for good.

Oz spotted his home as soon as he rounded the last curve. The glow from the thousands of Christmas lights used to decorate his place for Christmas could be seen a mile from his driveway. The open pasture provided a perfect view of the entire farm. Everything from the mailbox to small bushes lining the driveway up into the tip-tops of trees sparkled with an array of colors.

He glanced over at Liz. "We're here."

"That's your place?" Her gaze darted from one lit item to the next.

"In all the excitement of the night, I forgot to tell you. My wife, Roni, loved Christmas lights, and we started this tradition during our first season after we were married."

He turned down the drive and pulled up to the house. An assortment of colored lights lined the exterior from the ground floor all the way to the roof. Dozens of inflatable characters dotted the landscape from waving snowmen to Santa's reindeer dancing into the air.

"What do you think?"

Her hesitation wasn't a good sign. Most people either loved the display or saw it as a nuisance. Since he didn't have many neighbors, Oz didn't have to worry about the latter.

"I'm still trying to take it all in. It's a bit overwhelming. I don't know where to look first."

Other people's opinions didn't really matter because every time he pulled into the drive, joy filled him. This was a way to honor the memory of his wife. To keep a little bit of her during the holiday season.

"Roni called this our redneck Christmas. People from all over drive here for a visit." He rolled down the window. "And we have a soundtrack. Hear it?"

Speakers played a familiar carol to accompany the light show. Santa Claus was coming to town in this selection.

"I do."

"And I can even make the lights dance to the rhythm. Watch."

Oz scrolled to an app on his phone and tapped the screen. The current song changed to an orchestrated version of electric guitars, heavy drums and violins that set the lights into a syncopated frenzy. One of his favorites.

"Sometimes I change up the music when a large group of people arrive, and they will get out and dance in my driveway. You'd be surprised what some people will do when they are having a good time."

"I think I've forgotten how to have fun. I'm typically content with quiet nights and no drama."

Oz stopped the borrowed SUV in the middle of his drive and pointed outside. "Would you like to dance? The lights have a way of cheering people up when you're right in the middle of them all."

His heart raced as he waited for an answer. He'd not been so bold since he first asked Roni out. Back then, he was shy, but something drew him to his wife, and the same feeling stirred within him when he was around Liz.

She held his gaze for a moment longer. "I'm really exhausted. Rain check?"

He tapped his thumbs against the steering wheel for a moment, then rolled forward toward his detached garage and pressed the opener. Probably for the best. He didn't need to complicate their professional relationship. "Sure."

"I can honestly say, I've never seen anything quite like it, and I have to admit the display does have a soothing effect. Once a girl takes it all in. And it's a lot to take in."

Oz pulled the SUV inside. "Didn't your family decorate for Christmas?"

"Sure, but nothing like this. My mom's tastes were a bit more subdued. One tree lit up in the living room and maybe a wreath on the door or candles in the windows."

"Well, that sounds boring." He grabbed her bag from the floor and hopped out. "Follow me, and I'll show you your room."

They made their way through his Christmas obstacle course of a yard, past the pool and entered his home. He didn't bother to turn on any lights in the main living area. None were needed with the exterior glow shining through the large front windows and back patio doors.

He led her down a hallway where three bedrooms boasted his wife's feminine touches. He hadn't had the heart to change anything, and in some ways, he wondered if that kept him from moving forward. Every nook, corner and shelf held memories of Roni.

"This house just continues forever, doesn't it?" Liz's question pulled him from the past.

"Four bedrooms and three baths. About three thousand square feet in total. We have a pool out back and a covered outdoor kitchen area."

"We?"

He'd done it again. Even after five years, he still considered his wife when describing their home. "Sorry. Old habit."

"Oh. No worries."

They passed by his office. Old case file folders covered every surface, including all the information he kept on his brother. Every year he vowed to digitize his case records, but he preferred to hold the documents and photos in hand. Maybe he just didn't like change even though he'd purchased a state-of-the-art computer system. One of his buddies at the department built and programmed the device with extra firewalls and cybersecurity options to discourage hackers. He'd placed a monitor on the wall that was large enough for his blurry eyesight to read without glasses.

Liz stopped at the door. "Nice portrait."

He didn't even have to look at the eleven-by-fourteen wall photo to know which one she meant. He stared at it every day, remembering the good times with his arm wrapped around his stunning wife who was supposed to grow old with him. He'd convinced himself he'd never find another woman like her again.

Oz kept moving, entered the last bedroom and placed Liz's bag by the door. "This is you."

She walked past him into the room, taking in the surroundings. It felt weird to have her there, but it was only for one night until they could go to the lake cabin.

"I hope a king-size bed is okay. Got a comfy mattress, for sure."

She faced him. "As exhausted as I am, I'd take an old hard couch. I could sleep on anything right now."

"I have one of those too, in the basement."

Her laugh was warm and subtle. "Funny." She pointed

to the window. "Oh, thank goodness. You have black-out curtains. I was wondering how I was going to sleep with all the outside lights."

"Of course." He motioned to a door across the room. "That bath is all yours. Clean towels are in the closet. Sorry the room's not larger, but it's only for one night."

"I'll be fine. Thank you, Oz. I really appreciate it."

He shoved his hands in his pockets. "If you need anything, just text me. My suite's on the other end of the house so this entire end is empty. We——" He stopped at his mistake. "I bought the place, hoping to have a family, but that didn't work out."

She stepped closer and placed a hand on his arm. "Roni gave you both a lovely home. I'm grateful to have such a nice place to sleep tonight."

Her kind words about Roni drew heat to his face. "There are waters in the bottom drawer of the fridge if you need something to drink before bed. Good night."

She closed the door between them, and he stood in the hallway a moment longer. The woman stirred up feelings he wasn't ready to acknowledge. She'd be easy to fall for, and he'd have to keep his desires in check. Distractions in their line of work got people killed. His first priority was her safety, but that wouldn't be easy when her kind nature reminded him so much of his wife.

Liz leaned against the closed bedroom door in an effort to calm her racing heart. Oz's shy smile and blushed dimpled cheeks made her want to kiss him, not send him off with a simple good-night. What was she doing?

After everything she'd been through in her past, and even now, the last thing she needed was a romantic entanglement, especially with a man at work. Hadn't she learned her lesson with Trey?

She came to Mills Creek to put the pieces of her life back together before traveling down the road of love again. At least her job gave her the focus and time she needed to heal all the scars he'd left on her body and soul.

Liz walked to the bathroom and splashed cold water on her face, inspecting the bruises the intruder had left behind. Wasn't the first time she'd been hit, but at least this time her injuries were from the hands of a stranger.

She lifted her phone and looked at the recent text still displayed on her screen. Her ex-boyfriend's name loomed at the top—Trey McManus, Homicide Detective, Charlotte PD.

His new message haunted her, but not because of the contents. All he wanted was to talk, but conversations with Trey often turned into a violent game. One she had no desire to play anymore.

Sweat dripped down Oz's back when he sat up in bed, his heart racing from the nightmare. The clock displayed 5:00 a.m. in bright green numbers. He wanted to pull the duvet back over his head but something woke him up and he wasn't sure what.

He flung back the covers and let his legs hang over the side of the mattress, trying to gain his bearings. He wore the same clothes from earlier except for his socks and shoes, which he'd kicked onto the floor before crashing in bed. Not even the dried blood on his shirt deterred him.

He rubbed a hand over his eyes and sat waiting for the noise to sound again. After everything they'd been through in the last twenty-four hours, Oz couldn't take any chances, and he regretted not making the long drive to the lake cabin. At least there, they'd be farther from town.

Another soft clink resonated from the main living area. Possibly a turned lock or a tap against a window. He pulled up his security camera on his phone and checked all four. He didn't see anyone skulking around his home but decided to text Liz just in case.

Are you up?

She didn't answer. Probably still asleep unless an intruder had gotten to her first without him knowing.

Cold hardwood floors chilled his bare feet as he lifted his gun from the nightstand and pulled back the blackout curtain, allowing the glow of his outside lights to illuminate a slivered path to the door. He didn't have the luxury of waiting. Not with someone wanting to kill her.

Another thump prompted him to step into the short hallway. He leaned against the wall until he reached the corner. The kitchen was on the other side and then the living room. Oz stepped into view, his weapon aimed.

Liz froze in front of him, dropping her plastic cup. Cold water doused his pant legs, and pieces of ice scattered across the floor. He dropped his arms to his side, an instant wave of relief washing through him. "You scared me."

"Sorry. I was trying to be quiet." She grabbed a piece of ice near her foot and tossed it into the kitchen sink.

"Is everything okay?"

"I woke up and couldn't go back to sleep. So I decided

to get some water to keep my mind from playing every scenario of Tillie's murder over and over in my head."

"Were you not able to find the bottled waters?"

"I found them but I like ice water best."

Oz placed his weapon on the counter, grabbed a couple of towels from the drawer and knelt to clean up the spill.

Liz joined him. "I'm sorry about the mess."

"It's fine." Her toenails were painted a deep red, matching the font of her rock band T-shirt. "We need to get an early start anyway, if we want to get settled into your father's lake cabin before the sun comes up."

"You think we'll be safe there?"

"As safe as any other place. I'll just be glad to have you away from town. So far, the attempts on your life have centered here, and I hope they won't follow us farther out. We need to be extra cautious until we catch the person behind the hit."

She straightened and dropped a couple more ice cubes in the sink. "How are we going to do that if we're hiding? Maybe we should rethink our strategy."

Oz stood and twisted the rags into the sink, then draped them over the side to let them dry. "What do you mean?"

"I've done a lot of undercover work with Narcotics. Let's use my experience, set him up and draw this person into the open."

"This is not some street-level drug mule we're dealing with. This is a trained assassin coming for you."

"What do you think every member of a drug cartel is? They all carry guns, and the majority of them had to kill, assault or beat someone just to get into the gang.

I'm good at my job, and we'll have them in no time, if you'll agree to a sting operation."

No doubt her reputation preceded her abilities to bring down some of the most notorious kingpins in the area, which was even more of a reason to keep her from a risky decision like putting herself in the line of fire.

"We need more information before we dangle you on the carrot string for an assassin to shoot. We do this by the book and follow the guidelines. That way we keep you alive and bring in the person who's bankrolling the attempts on your life."

Liz folded her arms and leaned against the sink. "So—you're one of *those*."

"What do you mean?"

"The kind of cop that always follows the rule book and policies down to the last letter. Sometimes the best decisions are based on instinct."

"I thought we settled this already. I'm not taking any chances on getting you killed. Some of our best detectives have died—"

Glass shattered around them and pelted the side of Oz's face. He dove on top of Liz, and they fell to the floor. Warm blood from his previous gash dripped onto her T-shirt, spreading through the light gray fabric threads. "Are you hit?"

She shook her head and curled into him when more machine gunfire erupted from outside the home, blasting through the walls. Oz remained low but grabbed his gun from the countertop as Liz crawled into the short hallway, lifting her head to glance through a side window. "Three armed men. Two o'clock across the street. They're headed this way."

"We need to get you out of here."

"Or we can fight back, take at least one of them in and find out who's behind this."

"We don't have that kind of firepower. We need to leave. If we go through my bedroom's patio doors, we can get to the detached garage at the back of the house."

"I can't go outside in this." She pointed at the T-shirt and shorts she wore along with her bare feet. "I'll freeze."

The trek to the guest bedroom wasn't an option. Too many windows and glass already covered the floor in that direction. So much for grabbing her bag. Oz looked back over his shoulder to the bedroom he used to share with his wife. He'd never removed Roni's clothes. Hadn't had the heart to part with her things, even after five years. Oz took Liz's hand, pulled her into the suite and motioned toward the walk-in closet. "You're about Roni's size. Go see what you can find that fits and hurry."

She stared at him for a moment, recognition of his sacrifice displayed in her eyes. "Are you sure?"

"I'll keep guard, and when you're done changing, bring my brown hiking boots and a pair of socks with you."

Liz disappeared, and Oz moved to his standing gun safe kept in the corner. He pulled out two extra Glocks, another 9mm and several magazines. They'd need plenty of ammunition to make it off his property alive. He found a dry pair of jeans and swapped them out with the wet ones he wore now.

"Ready." She stepped from his closet and handed him the items he'd requested. He stared at her for a moment—a pang of reminiscence mixed with regret washed through him. She looked beautiful in Roni's jeans, hiking boots and lined leather jacket. He stepped forward and fingered the red scarf tied around Liz's neck. His wife always did look good in the deeper shade.

"Scarves keep me warm. Is it okay if I wear it?" Liz asked.

Oz lifted his gaze to hers. "Of course."

He dropped his hand to the boots she'd brought for him and slipped his feet inside. "I bought the scarf for Roni during our fifth anniversary. We went on a cruise to Alaska, and she'd forgot to pack hers. A week after we came home, my brother took her life."

"I can get another if you like. She had several."

"There's no time." He finished tying his boots, then crossed the room. "Let's go."

Oz pulled back the curtain and scanned the side yard. The detached garage was about five hundred feet away. A fenced-in patio area surrounded their pool and provided a bit of cover until they could reach the gate on the opposite side from their current location. As long as no one entered before they breached the gate, then they could get to the SUV unseen.

Gunfire erupted at the front entrance. Their attackers were inside. He pulled Liz through the door and into the cold night air. There was no way Oz was going to let another woman die in his home.

FOUR

Liz wove in between the lighted inflatable snowmen swaying on the back patio, thankful for a bit of Christmas cover. She ran around the side of Oz's pool topped with an old blue tarp fastened by a couple hooks that had seen better days. When she reached the back gate and pulled the handle, the latch caught. Oz's footsteps slapped the concrete behind her as voices from inside his home shouted commands, including her name. No question she was their target.

One kill shot out the back patio door and her life would be over.

The space where she stood exposed her to a sniper's sight line, and except for the privacy fence around the perimeter of the pool, the area was an open range. She and Oz were sitting ducks ripe for two bullets to take them out.

She tried the latch again and fumbled.

"Here, let me." Oz pulled her hand away and jimmied the latch loose. "It sticks."

"Thanks."

The gate opened inward, and a large man burst through, pushing the door and knocking Oz to the ground. One strong hand tightened on Liz's throat, while the other knocked the gun from her grip. She stumbled backward and fought to breathe. He squeezed tighter.

Cold black eyes stared at her as she clawed his fingers. Her boots slid backward across the concrete until he plunged her body into the pool, cover and all. The tarp collapsed and icy water enveloped her, shocking all her vital organs. She struggled against his hold, but his strong arm held her under.

The lack of oxygen burned her lungs as she fought against him. Her arms grew numb, tangled in the plastic, and the effects of hypothermia and drowning spiraled together in one toxic combination.

Dear, God—please don't let me die. Not like this.

A muffled gunshot fired, and the man's grip loosened. His body fell on top of hers, plunging her deeper into the pool, and stained the water red. She kicked with all her might and used what little strength she had left to rise to the top. Strong hands grabbed her shoulders and scraped her onto the concrete.

Oz knelt, his eyes wide with fear, and scooped her into his arms. "I've got you."

He rushed through the gate before the other assailants found them outside. She trembled against him in the cold night air, unable to warm her body, craving the heat from his skin.

"We need to get you warm."

She leaned her head into his chest, still shaking against him. "So cold."

The detached garage wasn't far, and they slipped in through the side door unnoticed. It wouldn't take long for the hostile men to find their buddy floating in the pool and they'd follow, even more determined to carry out their evil intentions.

Oz placed her in the passenger's seat. "Once I start this car, they'll know where we are."

She nodded, but all she could think about was the aching pain her body inflicted every time her muscles contracted trying to create heat. Oz turned the heater knobs on high, pointed every vent in her direction and wrapped a blanket from the back seat around her. With a turn of the key, gradually the cold air turned to hot and blasted through the slats. She curled into a ball, absorbing as much warmth as possible.

"Stay down."

She couldn't move if she tried except for the uncontrollable trembling her body refused to surrender.

Oz punched the garage door opener and hit the gas. Gunfire pelted the outside of the vehicle. Liz bounced in the seat and braced herself as he swerved onto the main road. After several minutes of defensive driving, Oz placed a hand on her wet head. "I think we've lost them."

Her body relaxed, the shivers slowed and she straightened in the seat. "Are you sure?"

"I don't think they followed. At least, not yet. I took several back roads. We're good for the moment."

He flinched when he reached to adjust one of the vents. Blood stained the sleeve of his shirt and Liz pulled his jacket back from his shoulder. "You've been shot."

"Just a graze. Stray bullet got me."

"There's a convenience store about another mile up the road. Friends of mine own it. Stop there so we can take care of your wound before it gets infected."

"It's too risky to stop. I'm fine."

"You're not fine."

"Neither are you. Your lips are still blue. You might want to remove the jacket, scarf, boots and socks to help you warm up faster."

She peeled off the wet articles and placed them in the back seat, then put her bare toes against the vents. "I'm sorry about your wife's clothes."

He gave a little shrug. "I'm glad we had them. I've been meaning to pack them up but never took the time."

"I guess that was a good thing for us tonight. Otherwise, I'd be wearing men's jeans, boots three sizes too big and socks that reached the top of my thigh."

"That would be a sight."

His laugh calmed the anxiety coursing through her. She hadn't spent much time with Oz since starting her narcotics job, and despite their current circumstances, he held an inner joy and strength, unlike her ex.

"Please stop at the store," Liz said. "I'll be quick. We can grab a few supplies and continue to my father's lake cabin."

"Two minutes. Can I park behind the store?"

"Yeah, there's a short alleyway."

The Boat Stop sat on a small hill off the main road and boasted four pumps made to resemble vintage gas tanks but with modern digital features. Liz's friend, Teya Bergen, was a retired trauma nurse from Charlotte and had moved to Mills Creek with her husband ten years ago to run their farm and store.

"She always keeps a stocked medical supply cabinet," Liz said when Oz pulled next to a dumpster at the back of the building. "I guess old tricks are hard to let go." She hopped out of the SUV and waited for him to enter with her.

The smell of coffee wafted through the air. Liz spotted her friend behind the café counter and waved when she looked up.

"Oh, my goodness. It's about time you made another trip to see me."

Liz hugged her friend.

"Why is your hair cold and wet?"

"Long story." Liz motioned to Oz who had zipped his outer jacket to hide the blood on his shirt. "Have you got somewhere we can go to talk in private?"

"Sure. I've got a break room. Follow me." Teya removed her apron and wiped her fingers on a dish towel. "Honey, I'm headed into the back."

Teya's husband shouted an acknowledgment from across the room, even though he wasn't visible. Liz tilted up on her toes. "Hi, Wallis."

His head popped up over one of the aisle shelves. "Liz. It's good to see you again. I'll come chat more in a minute. I'm right in the middle of inventory."

"Sounds good."

She and Oz followed Teya through a solid wooden door into a back hallway with a staff-only bathroom, a nice-sized storage room and into the break room decked out with a large sectional couch, oversize TV screen, kitchenette and table.

Teya took a seat. "What brings you to my neck of the woods?"

Liz nodded toward Oz, who paled more with every passing moment. "He's been shot."

Her friend popped up from the couch and transitioned into nursing mode. "Here, sit down. Let me take a look."

Within minutes, Teya had Oz's jacket off, shirtsleeve cut and Betadine swabs out. "What kind of trouble have you gotten yourself into now, Liz?"

"Nothing we can't handle as cops."

"Someone wants her dead." Oz flinched when Teya pressed on the wound.

"Sorry. There's some debris inside and cleaning the injury might hurt a little. Once that's done, then I can bandage the area. You'll need some antibiotics. I've got a doctor friend I'll call to get you a prescription. He owns a pharmacy in the strip mall just up the road." Teya kept working. "Who wants you dead, Liz?"

"Not sure exactly, but all this is tied to my CI's murder."

Her friend paused. "So they're coming for you too?"

"Looks that way."

Teya pointed at the table. "Hand me the sterile water bottle right there."

Liz did as instructed and admired her friend's skills. "Do you ever miss nursing?"

"Sometimes, but life is good here too. I like the slower pace and working for myself." Teya cleaned the wound more when the entrance tone for the store sounded. Everyone paused.

"When do you open?" Oz asked.

"Fifteen minutes." Teya secured tape to the bandage and stood. "And we typically don't get customers this early. Let me see who's out there."

Liz touched her friend's arm. "Don't tell anyone we're here."

"I won't. As long as Wallis hasn't done so already." Teya tossed the wrappers and used cleaning supplies into the trash before moving to the door. "There's a back exit at the end of this hallway that leads into the alley. I'll text you if I think you're in danger. Stay safe, friend."

Teya gave Liz a quick hug before she disappeared

back out front. Oz slipped his jacket back on and checked his weapon. "I'm getting low on ammunition. Do you still have my spare on you?"

"Left it in the car, but if I know Teya, she's got a gun around here somewhere." Liz searched through drawers and cabinets, then walked down the short back hall to the storage room with Oz. Her phone buzzed.

Leave now. They have your photo.

"We've gotta go. It's them."

"They'll see us pull out. We have to wait and pray they haven't found our SUV at the back."

Liz closed the storage door and locked the dead bolt. Male voices echoed from the hallway, and then she heard Teya. "I told you no one's back here." Wallis let out a loud groan. "Please don't hurt him. We're telling you the truth."

"Then you won't mind if we look."

Liz and Oz moved to the back of the storage room behind a rack of boxed supplies. She wanted to kick herself for not bringing the extra gun with her. She peeked in several of the boxes. One held an assortment of kitchen knives. She grabbed the largest she could find. Better than nothing.

The door handle jiggled. "Why's this locked?" the man asked.

"It's the maintenance room, and the property manager who owns the building doesn't want us going in there. Said if we have any problems to call him."

Liz hated she'd placed her friend in danger but was thankful for her quick thinking skills.

"You're lying. I know they've been here. There's

bloody gauze pads in the trash. So tell me where they are or hubby gets it again."

"How are we supposed to know?"

Another groan from Wallis. "Okay. Don't hurt him. I'll tell you. They headed back toward town."

A loud thump hit the wall, and Teya screamed for the man to stop. "You better not be lying or you won't like it when we return."

Footsteps stomped away from the room, and the chime sounded upon their exit. Liz turned the door lock, stepped into the hallway and found her friend seated on the floor next to her injured husband.

Liz rushed to his side. "Are you okay?"

A purple bruise formed around his swollen eye. "I will be."

Teya motioned toward the break room. "He needs ice."

"I'll get some." But before Liz made her way to the door, Oz emerged, cold pack in hand. She hadn't even seen him walk off.

He handed her friend the bag. "We'll give them time to leave the area, then head on to the lake cabin. You did good, Teya. Especially sending them in the opposite direction. That should buy Liz and me some time to get to our destination without being followed."

"Thanks." She placed the cool bag against her husband's face.

Liz knelt beside her and squeezed her free hand. "I'm so sorry. We shouldn't have come here."

"Yes, you should've, and we'd help you again a million times over. Now, get out of here before they come back."

The burn of familiar tears stung Liz's eyes. She didn't

want to leave her friend after the trauma she'd caused, but they had no other choice.

Oz held out his hand and helped her to her feet. "She's right. We need to go."

Liz gave Teya another hug and promised to call when they arrived safely, then slipped out the back door and into the SUV.

He handed her his phone. "If you don't mind, will you enter the location to your dad's place?"

Tears blurred her vision, and she wiped her eyes. "Can't. There isn't one. Dad had the lake address erased from all maps on the internet."

"How'd he manage that?"

"He knows some of the best cybersecurity agents in the country and hates the internet. He called in a favor or two."

Liz motioned for him to take a left onto a back road, then popped open the glove box and retrieved a napkin and pen to jot down the directions. "This should get you close. I'm exhausted. Wake me up when you get to the strip mall." She leaned her seat back.

"Before you fall asleep, I've been wanting to ask you something."

"Make it quick. I'm fading fast."

"You said something about a bad breakup. What happened?"

A long car ride to a lake cabin in the woods was the perfect time to discuss her painful past relationship with Trey, but she avoided the details even with her closest friends, much less a man she'd officially met less than twenty-four hours ago. Her loved ones had tried to help her when things turned bad, and being a cop, she knew better—even received training to help women in similar situations. How was she supposed to tell Oz she chose to stay with a man who almost killed her on multiple occasions?

He wouldn't understand. Her past was better left hidden away, undiscussed, especially since every time she packed her bags to leave, Trey had convinced her to stay or threatened her family. The man knew how to fill her mind with terror, and only when her cousin showed up and dragged her out was she able to leave town and escape the vicious cycle. Nightmares and paralyzing fear still plagued her at times, but with a new job and home, she didn't want to return to those dark memories.

"You know how it goes. Girl meets boy, falls head over heels in love and then boy breaks the girl's heart. Let's just say I've lived that scenario."

"I guess." He looked over at her. "When you mentioned it before, there seemed to be more to it than that."

She wasn't ready for this discussion. Not with Oz or any of her other colleagues. At least not yet. Her phone vibrated with a message from Teya. "Wallis is doing better and wants to know how your arm feels."

"Sore."

Liz pointed at the road. "The strip mall is up ahead. Teya's doctor friend said he'd meet us with your antibiotic." She shifted in her seat and rested her head against the window, hoping her body language communicated the end of their conversation.

"You didn't really answer my question."

"I know." She glanced back over her shoulder and nodded toward the speedometer. "If you don't step on the gas, we'll miss our meeting. Doc only has about fifteen minutes before his first appointment."

Oz lifted his hand and looked at the gauges, then

pressed the gas a bit more. She closed her eyes and prayed Trey left her alone. Maybe she should tell Oz about the text she received from him. If only she could be sure the nightmare she lived through wouldn't come back to haunt her. Her ex didn't typically hide in the shadows or conduct secret attacks. No—he came at her full force with his intent to harm clear in his dark eyes. The fact that she was still alive proved he didn't know where she was. At least not yet. Otherwise, she'd be the one lying on a metal slab in the morgue.

The Lake Marie Marina stretched out before Oz and hundreds of luxury boats bobbed up and down on the smooth water. The boardwalk boasted aluminum decking and every dock extension was covered with a sturdy metal roof. He'd never seen a marina as fancy as this one.

Gray clouds rolled across the sky and freezing rain spit against his face. He picked up his pace. "We better hurry or we're gonna get wet."

Liz raised a hand and motioned to the next row. "The slip is number 254."

He boarded the nice Master Craft speedboat Liz pointed out while she untied the ropes. Oz found the key in a small compartment near the driver's seat. "Sweet. This thing is nice."

"Dad bought this about a year before he retired."

Liz stepped into the hull and took a seat. "Have you driven a boat before?"

"Of course. My uncle and I used to go fishing all the time. He let me drive."

"Great. Then head out to the main water and take a right. I'll guide you from there."

The winds increased and brought heavy rain as they

moved down the lake. Oz fought to maintain control as they bounced across the choppy waters toward Liz's lake cabin.

He was thankful for the dose of antibiotics and ibuprofen the doctor gave him. Most of his pain had subsided for the moment. Now, if only he had something to eat and a bed. That would be helpful. They both needed rest.

Oz swiped a hand across his face and pushed the gas lever forward. Mountains surrounded them, and the dense fog hindered his visibility. Spurts of rain needled his face and arms, soaking them both to the core again. Cold winter temperatures and freezing wind threatened hypothermia and frostbite. Especially for Liz. This was the second dose of icy water chilling her to the bone.

He hoped once they were inside, warm and fed, she'd open up about her past. Her avoidance of the subject made him nervous. He didn't like secrets, especially if she was distracted by them during a case. Most likely, Tillie was killed by a drug cartel member and Oz needed Liz to be at her best.

But right now, his first priority was finding this cabin and shielding her from the rain or anything else that could harm her.

Liz shivered next to him as strong winds assaulted them from all sides. She needed heat from a fireplace, blankets and some warm soup or coffee for an extended period of time. If her father's cabin was outfitted like she'd mentioned, then he'd find all three.

"Take a left at that opening up ahead." Her fingers shook when she pointed out the direction. "We're almost there."

He steered the boat into a hidden cove and toward a

large covered dock with a cupola and weathervane on top. The house sat tucked among the evergreen trees almost hidden from view. Oz pulled the gas throttle back then cut the engine and let the boat drift onto a lift underneath the sheltered area.

Liz hopped off the craft, secured the boat and raised her arms as if welcoming an old friend. "This is it."

Vaulted support beams exposed spiderwebs and remnants of bird nests from the summer season. The modern decking appeared brand new and displayed little wear from use. Maybe her father didn't come here much anymore.

Liz turned and pointed toward an inclined slope. "The house is just up the hill."

As Oz walked along the inclined concrete path, he caught glimpses of the home through the tree branches. A far cry from the dirt trail at his uncle's cabin. He'd spent several months there after he emerged from rehab. The two-room structure gave him a quiet place to grieve his wife's death and heal with days of fishing, boating and spending time with God. The place was small and nothing like the mansion rising before him.

The trees parted and the rain eased into a sprinkle, exposing a large stone-and-wood-framed house perched atop a cleared acre of land with a rock chimney rising up the middle. The place was huge.

Oz stopped walking and peered up at the three-story structure. "Your idea of a lake cabin and mine are very different."

Liz followed his gaze. "What did you think it was going to be?"

"Smaller. Like two rooms, not fifteen. This is not a cabin. It's a mansion."

"Some of my best memories are from spending time here as a kid. We'd ride jet skis and tube behind my dad's boat. We loved to stay out on the water all day."

"And you don't anymore?" Oz grabbed a couple of logs stacked against the basement wall while Liz unlocked the door. He'd make a fire as soon as they got inside.

"I still like to go for boat rides but all the jarring from tubing and skiing are a bit much for me these days." She pointed at the logs in his hand. "What are you doing?"

"You'll need a fire to get warm once we're inside."

She smiled at him. "Those logs are for the outdoor firepit. The interior fireplace is gas. All we have to do is flip a switch."

"Good to know." Oz returned the logs to the stack, a bit embarrassed, and followed her inside.

The finished basement of the home boasted a large game room, kitchenette and two bedrooms off to the side with their own attached baths. Liz led him up a wooden staircase to the main level. Large floor-to-ceiling windows stretched above vaulted wooden beams and flanked the stone fireplace he'd seen from the outside. The masonry work was the main attraction of the open room until the sunrise streaked across the mountains.

"What do you think?" Liz flipped the switch to the fireplace, igniting instant heat, and turned the settings to high. A glow cast around her. Gorgeous. She belonged in this luxurious home.

He took a step back and focused on the flames. "It'll do."

She grabbed a couple of blankets from a large basket and tossed one to him. "Take your coat and boots off. We need to get warm."

Oz didn't hesitate and peeled off his outer layers,

pulling a couple of the leather armchairs closer so they would be comfortable.

Heat from the fireplace soon warmed the room. The pink blush of Liz's cheeks and lips returned. She curled up in the leather chair and ran her fingers along the edge of her blanket while the morning sun stretched through the window and streaked her face.

He wanted to place his lips against hers, but instead, he stood and turned toward the kitchen. "Got any coffee?"

"There should be some in the cabinet above the coffee maker. I keep the place stocked with staple items, and coffee is something a kitchen should never be without."

Oz made a pot and searched the pantry for something to eat. "Looks like all you've got for breakfast is a box of protein bars, some cans of chicken noodle soup and a pack of beef jerky."

"I'll take a bar." She leaned forward to catch the one he tossed across the room.

"It's not my amazing three-egg omelet, but these will give us calories and energy. If I had all the ingredients, I promise I would cook a breakfast like you've never had before."

Liz unfolded from her chair and joined him in the kitchen as he filled a mug for her. She stepped close to his side and peered at him over the rim of her mug, green eyes finding his, long dark hair falling to her chest. "What would you cook me?"

Heat surged through him, and he diverted his gaze, stepped to the other side of the island and leaned against the countertop. "We'd have a full spread—southwestern omelets, pancakes with fresh strawberries and bacon, of course."

"Of course." She flashed a smile, weakening his resolve to remain professional, then moved around the island and took a seat on a bar stool next to him. "When this is over, I'm going to hold you to that promise, Detective."

His gaze drifted to her lips, and for a moment, he let himself wonder what it might be like to kiss her, to hold a woman in his arms again. The last time had been far too long ago.

But distractions were how cops got killed, and he needed all his wits about him with assassins on their tail. Oz lifted his mug and drained the rest of his coffee, then returned to the fireplace for his boots. She did the same, then placed a hand on his arm.

He paused. Her fingers slipped into his hand, giving him a slight tug.

"Come on." She tilted her head toward the back of the house. "I'll show you Dad's security room."

They passed a couple of bedrooms, a half bath and a theater room before Liz stopped in the middle of the hallway. She faced one of the paneled inlays lining the corridor, the master suite to their right.

Oz peeked into the bedroom, then back to her as she pulled her phone from her pocket and scrolled through the screens.

"How did your cell survive the pool?" he asked.

"Waterproof case. Believe it or not, I've lost a couple of phones to water damage. I left one out in the rain, and then another fell into a place at the airport I'd rather not discuss."

"Gross."

"Tell me about it. Thankfully it was an early flight and the bathrooms had just been cleaned."

She pushed against an inlay and released, opening a hidden compartment with a digital screen inside. Liz typed in the security code and let the device scan her index finger before an interior door slid open. Oz followed her inside.

Automatic lights triggered with the motion and highlighted built-in shelving units, cabinets and drawers filled with an array of weapons. From Glocks to 9mm and AR-15s, this room was an officer's dream.

He opened one of the drawers. "Are these real grenades?"

"Yeah. Dad kept a stocked supply of military-grade weapons here."

"No wonder he doesn't want to have his location on the grid."

"There are smoke bombs in there too. Might be helpful to give us cover if we need to escape."

Liz moved to the back of the room and flipped on several computer monitors. The screens initialized and connected to eight security cameras positioned around the perimeter of the home. "Now we'll be able to see if anyone's coming. That'll give us time to gear up and move out if needed. Alarms are automatically set to alert us to any intrusions."

Her phone vibrated on the counter beside them and

displayed the name of the caller. Liz flipped the screen face-down, her body tense.

"Who's Trey?"

She pulled out a chair and busied herself scrolling through the different camera angles. "No one."

Oz had interrogated enough criminals to know when someone was hiding a secret. "Is he the person who texted you before?"

Liz ignored his question and his suspicions rose. "You can either tell me who this man is or I can do some digging on my own. One way or the other, I need to know if he's going to be a problem for our case."

She leaned in closer to the monitor screen as if she didn't hear a word he said, clicked the mouse and magnified the image.

"He's my ex but not a threat." Liz stood from her chair and faced him. "Besides, we've got other problems." She pointed to one of the screens. "They're here."

Men jumped from a docked boat and fanned out across the bottom of the hill. They ascended toward the house.

"That was quick." Oz turned back to the drawers and shelves to gather the weapons needed.

"They must've tracked my phone."

"Does anyone else know about this cabin?"

"Only Trey, my ex."

"Do you think he's behind any of this?"

"I doubt it. He didn't know Tillie and the attacks started with her murder. But since the hitmen were tracking Tillie and me, then they might've known about Trey too."

Liz crossed the room, slapped at a red button on the wall and the entrance closed off, locking behind her. She grabbed a couple of Glocks, loaded them with magazines and slipped on a shoulder holster.

"It's pretty isolated around here in the winter months. Most of the neighbors go home during the colder season."

"No neighbors make a hitman's job easier to carry out." Oz grabbed an AR-15 and a 9 mm, then opened a couple of drawers where an array of knives and other weapons were stored. He took two, grabbed a couple of grenades and moved back to the monitor screens where she stood. "Which way out?"

"They left two men in front of the boathouse and our tunnel exits right in front of them. They'll see us for sure."

"Two against two. I'll take those chances. Or we could stay here?"

"I'm not keen on being trapped in small spaces. I say we get out while we can. Let's take the tunnel."

Oz watched as the other four men breached the first-floor entrance. "I can't believe your dad built a tunnel."

Liz moved to a back cabinet and handed him a Kevlar vest, then pressed a button to a built-in elevator. "He was a bit paranoid. Rightfully so with the kind of military work he did. He wanted an escape route no one would suspect."

"I'm thankful for his paranoia."

"Follow me. This contraption will take us there."

Two metal doors opened in front of him. Oz donned

a bulletproof vest and stepped into the elevator, but Liz hesitated, remaining in the room. Her face paled.

"You coming? We don't have much time."

She inhaled a deep breath before moving inside, then gripped the handrail upon entry. Her knuckles turned white.

Oz punched the button to close the elevator doors and leaned against the wall as they descended. Liz squeezed her eyes shut. No wonder she took the stairs all the time.

"I'm guessing you don't like elevators?"

"It's not the elevator. It's the small, enclosed space."

"Have you always had this phobia?"

"Not exactly. This fear is a by-product of a past relationship. A little nugget I carry with me to this day."

"Good grief. What did Trey do to you?"

The elevator lurched to a stop, and she opened her eyes, meeting his gaze. "Let's just say alcohol made him angry. I'd lock myself in our small closet for hours until he passed out. Hence, the reason I hate small spaces. Not something I typically share with my colleagues."

Oz stood frozen for a moment. "He was that bad?"

"Bad enough."

White-hot rage spread through his body. If Oz ever got his hands on this guy, he'd make sure he understood the pain he'd inflicted on her. "No wonder you're avoiding his messages."

"I'm avoiding his messages because we're over. Not out of fear."

"But what if this isn't over? What if this isn't about Tillie but hurting you instead? Someone's trying to kill you, and if Trey's the kind of person who would hurt you when y'all were together, he could be the one driving this relentless pursuit now. How many assassins do you know that bring a whole army to an isolated lake house after a cop who witnessed their crime? Not many. In fact, most of them don't want to kill a cop because it brings to much heat down on their head and disrupts their business."

Liz stepped from the elevator as soon as the door opened. Oz followed. "This feels more personal to me."

"Okay. You have a point," She adjusted the straps on her Kevlar vest. "But we can't ignore the fact that Tillie died first. How does that fit into Trey's motive?"

"She got in the way."

If this *was* a personal vendetta launched at Liz, then they needed to change their approach to the case. "And you think Trey remembers the location of the lake house?"

"Yeah. We came here multiple times."

"Maybe now we know how they found us so quickly."

"He also knows the code to my dad's security room with the weapons cache."

The man had an advantage, and if Trey was behind this, then he'd be ready for them when they exited the tunnel.

How was Oz supposed to keep her safe if she didn't tell him everything, especially after he failed to do the same for the woman he'd loved all his life?

"This could all be him."

Liz moved farther into the damp, musty tunnel, then turned back to face him. "I disagree. The attack on Tillie is classic for a cartel hit. Somehow they must've discovered she was working with me. Trey's not behind this. It has to be someone else."

Dozens of questions invaded his mind about her past relationship, and he needed answers, but from her tone, he wasn't sure she'd be giving any. She might not think her ex was involved but he wasn't so sure and if he was behind the threats, then they could be walking right into a trap.

FIVE

Rats squeaked from the shadows of the tunnel, but Liz ignored the sounds and moved toward the entrance. A few rodents didn't bother her as long as she wasn't locked in a claustrophobic room with them.

Her father dug the underground escape route when she was a little girl and he was at the height of his military career. The man never spoke about his missions, but when she was older, he told her he was part of Special Forces and did a lot of things that still haunted him to this day. She never asked for details. The look in his eyes was enough for her.

She often wondered if the time he spent alone at the lake during his leave was a self-imposed solitary confinement to give him the ability to deal with the trauma of war. When she was little, she missed him during those weeks away, but now she understood he'd had no other choice.

After retirement, he moved to Florida, where he spent his days in the sun and deeded the lake property to her.

On more than one occasion, she'd retreated here but still thought of the place as her dad's. Maybe she'd join him one day in Florida for more than holiday visits, but for now the mountains were her home.

Oz lagged behind at the moment. Probably trying to calm his anger after her news about Trey. His face had turned red when he learned of the recent text the man sent. To be honest, the unexpected contact made her nervous also. She didn't trust Trey despite the apologetic tone of his message.

However, if this was her case and she was tasked with protecting someone, then finding out pertinent information after the fact would upset her too, but Oz didn't know the truth about Trey. Not yet, and now was not the time to share if she wanted them to get out of here alive.

A quick peek around the corner provided a line of sight to the men keeping watch along the shore. Anchored to her father's wooden dock was a couple of speedboats, bobbing up and down in the water. Each of the men remained behind the wheel, brandishing rifles. She flattened against the wall and ran through the best course of action in her mind.

Oz brushed her shoulder. "What's the verdict?"

"We got two hostiles on the dock. They're armed."

"Then we have a fighting chance." He held out his hand. "Here. I grabbed a couple of smoke grenades from your father's drawer. If we throw them both at the same time, that will give us a couple minutes to exit the tunnel and escape into the woods. What's the best path?"

"The dock is located to the left of the tunnel exit, so we should go right, then up the hill. A wooden shed sits halfway up. My neighbor uses the building to store his jet skis during the off season. They never come down in the winter. If we can get there before the smoke clears, we should have enough cover to make the trek to his home and slip inside without being noticed."

Oz nodded toward the smoke bomb still in his hand. "On my signal."

Liz took the device, pulled the pin and held the trigger in place. She removed her Glock with her free hand and waited for Oz to do the same. He motioned for release. They stepped around the corner in sync, threw the grenades at the boat and ran to the right.

Adrenaline fueled her legs as she raced up the hill. Smoke blurred her vision and burned her lungs. The assassins shouted commands and shot their weapons blind. Bullets whizzed around her. She pushed harder, the shed's outline just ahead.

More shadowed movement descended from the lake house and several men ran toward the dock. The dense smoke hid her from view.

Liz shot a few rounds to provide Oz with cover. Their attackers darted behind bushes, and she kept moving. If they could get to the dense tree line, then they had a chance.

Loose rock covered the increasing incline of the bank, and her boots slipped. She pitched forward and grabbed the shed's trim, unwilling to slide back into the line of fire. She pulled with her fingers and crawled behind the building to wait for Oz.

Seconds seemed like hours. The pops and pings of bullets hitting metal sounded behind her. With each passing moment, she grew more anxious. Oz hadn't shown.

Gunfire grew closer. She peeked around the edge. Oz stood behind a large tree with three men ascending on his position. His gaze met hers, and he shook his head. Liz flattened back into place. He needed her help. There was no way Oz could take on three gunmen by himself and live.

With a deep breath in, she rounded the corner, both guns raised, and fired. Oz held up his hand, yelled something inaudible, but she kept shooting. This gang wasn't going to take another person from her.

One of the assassins shifted his attention in her direction while the other two ran back down the hill. He aimed and fired. His bullet came hard and fast, hitting her center mass in the chest.

Instant pain seared through her sternum. The Kevlar vest she wore stopped the fatal injury, but the force of the hit radiated through her body. She fell to the ground, gasping for air, her weapon no longer in hand. Every breath increased her agony.

Sharp rocks cut into her palms as she tried to crab crawl back to cover. Torment seared through every motion. How could a projectile so small deliver such a strong punch? Black dots danced in the corners of her eyes, and a cold sweat dripped down her neck. She looked at Oz. His eyes were wide, and his lips mouthed her name.

Time slowed and raced by in unison. He pulled a pin and tossed a real grenade in the midst of her attackers. No smoke. Only fire and force.

Heat swallowed the chill of the day. Gunfire ceased, and the loud boom rattled the shed next to her. Flames crackled in the daylight, igniting one of the boats into a black-smoked inferno that choked out any breathable oxygen. The remaining attackers ran back to what was left of the dock.

Liz heaved and rolled to her side. Footsteps rushed toward her, then she was in Oz's arms, lifted and carried to safety. He placed her on the ground once they were behind the shed and ripped open her jacket.

His gentle hands pressed against her neck and chest, assessing her injuries. "The vest saved your life."

She peeled off the Kevlar, inciting pain with every move. "It hurts, that's for sure."

"You'll have one nasty bruise."

"Won't be the first time."

His lips pressed into a thin line with her comment, and he didn't respond. Instead, Oz slipped an arm around her waist and helped her to her feet. "Let's get inside, before they send in reinforcements."

A loud boom shook the ground, and debris shot into the sky. The boat on fire exploded and destroyed the rest of her father's dock. Several men jumped into the water and swam for the other craft trolling away from the area.

Liz looked back at her father's house. Shattered glass and chunks of the rock foundation littered the ground. She hoped the damage wasn't the same on the inside. "My dad's place is ruined."

"Insurance will cover it, but right now we've gotta move. Our location's been compromised."

"We can stay at the neighbor's house. They close it up for the winter. No one will expect us to remain in the area after all this."

"How are we gonna get in?"

"I know where they hide the spare key. We always check on each other's properties when we come down."

"I'll call Sergeant Wright once we're inside with an update. This team of assassins will be expecting us to return to a police safe house. Maybe we can figure out our next move and get ahead of this for a change."

"That would be nice."

"And don't think I've forgotten about your ex. We're going to talk about that too."

They made their way inside her neighbors' home, keeping the curtains closed and lights off. The storm had receded, and the interior brightened with sunshine. Someone had called the local fire department, who arrived at their secluded cove in well-equipped fire boats, blaring loud sirens and scaring off any remaining attackers. Before long the area crawled with men in yellow suits focused on extinguishing the blaze, but no one knocked on their door since the place appeared vacant from the outside.

Liz sank into a large sectional sofa and kept her movements minimal. The pain in her chest had eased a little but still pierced through her with each wrong twist.

Oz entered the room from a side hallway and handed her a bottle of ibuprofen. "Found this in the bathroom medicine cabinet. Should help."

"Thanks." She knocked back three without any water, then stretched out on the couch and stared at the coffered ceiling. The cozy living area boasted low beams with more rustic charm than her father's home. The owners had a rock fireplace too, tucked off to the side and surrounded by built-in bookcases with the latest reads and family photos. Any other day, she'd find a good book and get lost in a thrilling story, but after all the excitement they'd had, the only thing she wanted was sleep.

Liz took in a deep breath as her chest pain faded. "We're still no closer to finding out who killed Tillie. All this running and hiding isn't helping our case."

"But you're alive. That's what matters." Oz rummaged through the kitchen cabinets. "I'll build us a fire once the department leaves. The smoke will signal our location, and I think it's best if no one knows we're here until I make a full report to Sergeant Wright."

"Hiding out is useless." She flinched as she propped up on a pillow. "Maybe we should go back to the precinct, come up with a plan and use me as bait to draw out the moneyman. We could put out the word that my memory has returned or another rumor to entice a meeting."

He filled a kettle with water, placed it on the stove and removed a few tea bags from a container. "It's too risky."

"Not if we put a strike team together. I've done this a hundred times. Going undercover is part of what I do every day, and I'm good at it."

"Not gonna happen."

"But—"

"This is my case, and I'm not going to put you in danger like that. These people have almost taken your life more times than I can count."

The kettle began to whistle, and Oz turned off the burner. "If you don't want to run anymore, then I'll call WITSEC, but I'm not letting you martyr yourself."

He filled two mugs with the steaming drink and handed one to Liz, taking a seat next to her. She lifted the warm tea to her lips and formed an argument in her mind to save for Sergeant Wright. She'd call him for approval. He knew her capabilities and didn't let emotion or past tragedies cloud his judgment.

If Oz knew half the things she'd done at her former job in Charlotte, he'd be shocked. She regretted some of her decisions, but the streets were safer when risks were made to save lives. By putting herself in dangerous situations, top leaders were arrested, and narcotics rings stretching all the way to state government officials were stopped.

This scenario was no different. If she hid from every gun-toting criminal, she'd never have any successes or escaped her abusive ex. Trey had tried to control her life before, and she vowed to never let that happen again. Not even with Oz.

"This might be your case, but Tillie was my confidential informant, and I'll do whatever I can to find out who killed her. If I have to put myself out there to find her murderer, then so be it."

He sat back, a serious gaze falling on her once again. "Tell me about Trey."

Not the topic she wanted to discuss with the man who'd just made her so angry she could spit nails. "You don't need to worry about Trey. That's my personal life, and I can handle him."

"At least let me rule him out. Bronson can look into his movements and financials. If his messages are purely coincidental to the attacks on your life, then no harm done, right?"

"We need to be looking into the cases Tillie worked for me and her father's business dealings. If only I had my laptop." She took another sip of her tea and stood. "I'm going to take a shower."

"Liz—"

She pivoted to face him. "Trey's not the one trying to kill me."

"How can you be so sure?"

"Because the last time he hit me, I shot him, and now he's paralyzed from the waist down. He's in a wheelchair and struggles to live a normal life. The last thing he has time for amongst all his therapy and doctor's appointments is to send assassins after me. This has nothing to do with him."

Tears burned at the corners of her eyes, and she blinked them back. "Happy? Now you know all my dark secrets."

Liz entered the bedroom, closed the door behind her and leaned against the surface. Tears streamed down her cheeks. She'd almost killed Trey. Would have if her aim had been a little more to the left. The oath she took to protect lives and uphold the laws of North Carolina came crashing down around her in one horrific night.

The district attorney had ruled her actions as self-defense, but the guilt and stigma of ruining one of Charlotte PD's best homicide detectives ran her out of town. Trey had closed more murder cases than anyone in their precinct and was held in high esteem among their colleagues. Nothing was the same once she exposed the secrets of his abuse.

Needing a fresh start, she searched for a place to help her forget the past and start over, but who was she kidding? She couldn't outrun the trauma he caused or the sins of her choices. Memories of Trey's abuse haunted her every time she closed her eyes no matter where she lived. Their grip tightened around her mind with each passing moment. She slid to the floor and prayed for the ability to put her past behind her.

Now Oz knew the truth. Before long, every one of her new colleagues would know her secrets. That's how department gossip worked. They'd look at her with pity and treat her with kid gloves, just like Oz had done today— and that was worse than getting shot in the chest.

* * *

Oz downed the last of his tea and stared at the closed wooden door separating him from Liz. No wonder she left Charlotte and moved to Mills Creek. More than once he'd wanted to do the same thing. Escape all the reminders of his wife's death, but memories followed a person wherever they went, especially the bad ones.

He'd been fortunate to have only one kill to his name during his time on the Narcotics unit. The drug dealer had taken his partner hostage, and he never regretted his choice that night, but the death haunted him more than he admitted. He often had nightmares of the man's face, his blank stare looking straight at him.

He figured if he was going to dream about dead people, he might as well move to Homicide and bring some relief to other people's pain. But with Liz, he'd not brought relief. Instead of respecting her privacy, he pressured her into discussing her past. He owed her an apology.

Oz crossed the room and knocked. Her footsteps shuffled across the floor before the door opened. Her green eyes were rimmed red. He'd made her cry.

"I'm sorry. I should've trusted you about Trey. I wasn't trying to pry. I'm just the kind of person who needs all the information even when it's none of my business, and I pushed too hard."

She folded her arms and leaned against the frame. "You were only trying to help, and we need to look at every angle of the case. I would've done the same. I just know that Trey's not involved."

"Can we talk more about what happened with him?"

Liz moved back to the couch. "Trey wasn't violent when we first started dating, but his job took a toll after he worked the murder case of two children that went unsolved. He said he knew who killed them, but the evidence was thin and their father walked. The man was wealthy, had a mistress and an amazing legal team. They got the best evidence tossed on a technicality."

"We've seen that happen here too." Oz poured them two more mugs of hot tea. "There's nothing more infuriating than a judge throwing the case out when we work so hard to provide the evidence."

She took the mug from his hands. "He started drinking more after that. His way to cope or to forget what he'd seen. Truth was, I understood what he was going through. Probably even drew me closer to him because of it. He convinced me to move in with him. I'd stopped going to church, and my life with God had taken a back seat. I made some bad choices and gave in. Then his drinking became an every night occurrence."

"And he started hitting you?"

"The abuse was random at first. A hard shove during an argument or a tight neck grab from behind." She hugged a pillow to her chest. "Trey was smart enough not to hit me in the face but the rest of my body was his punching bag. In the winter, my clothes kept the bruises hidden from my colleagues but in the summer I had to cover the marks with tattoo makeup or long-sleeve shirts. I used to tell everyone I was cold-natured."

She paused. "After the case, things escalated. He became controlling and obsessive, drinking more and more. His job performance lagged, and he took his frustrations out on me. Things turned ugly."

Her shoulders lifted in a slight shrug. Tears filled her eyes again. "And then one night he came home and accused me of cheating. I thought he was going to kill me, and I grabbed my weapon. The rest you know."

Oz reached out and brushed her cheek with the back of his fingers. Her soft skin flushed with his touch. She carried a weight of undeserved guilt for protecting herself against a dangerous man. No one should have to experience what she'd endured.

"You know his injury is not your fault. He should've never placed a hand on you."

"My mind understands the logic behind my actions, but my heart still struggles. I almost killed someone I loved. We take an oath to protect and serve our communities, but I was willing to take his life."

"You weren't willing. He forced you to defend yourself. As cops, we make those split-second decisions every day. No one can understand how quickly death can happen until they are put in a similar situation. He made you choose—you or him."

"I was afraid to tell you."

"Why?"

"My former unit ostracized me after the shooting. They knew us both. We were a family, but when the time came, they took sides, and the majority chose Trey. That's why I left."

Oz took her hand and let his fingers tangle with hers. "I'm glad you came here."

She lifted her gaze and leaned closer. He didn't pull away this time but gave in to the desire to comfort and protect her.

Her lips brushed his, leaving behind the taste of peppermint lip gloss. She hesitated for a moment, as if unsure of his response, but he kissed her back, allowing emotions he hadn't felt in years to surface and fade the scars of his past.

"Wait." She moved back breathless.

He straightened. "Did I do something wrong? I apol—"

"It's not that." Liz stood for a moment and pushed her hair over her shoulder. "You did everything right. Maybe a little too right."

"Oh."

He didn't want to say the wrong thing or defuse the chemistry between them. Nor did he want her to walk away without ever kissing him again. She paced the floor for a few seconds and then sat in an opposing chair, keeping her distance.

"We shouldn't do this."

"I know it's been a while since I kissed a woman, but I thought there was something—" He really didn't want to tell her how great the kiss was, when she clearly regretted her decision. "I guess I'm confused."

She crossed her legs in the chair and brushed her long dark bangs from her face. With her cheeks flushed and her shirt a bit wrinkled, she met his gaze. "The kiss was good, but I've done the workplace romance before. Not that you're Trey, but I promised myself I wouldn't make the same mistake twice. Interoffice entanglements get messy."

"Just good, huh?"

Her head dipped slightly, but he caught the smile that reached her eyes. "Better than good."

He collected their tea mugs and moved to the kitchen with a bit of a sting to his ego. "I guess we need to set some professional boundaries between us then."

She crossed the room and took a seat on one of the island stools. "I just don't want a repeat in this department if things get weird between us. I've made some good friends since moving here and an interoffice romance could change the dynamic."

"And what makes you think things will get weird?"

"How many cops do you know who have successful relationships with a colleague?"

Oz tapped his fingers on the counter and tried to come back with one example of a successful interdepartmental relationship. They had none in their precinct.

Maybe she was right and they shouldn't get involved romantically. He pulled his phone from his pocket. "I need to call Bronson and Sergeant Wright and give them an update."

"About this?"

"Of course not. I don't kiss and tell." He stepped to the side, still annoyed with the situation, and tapped his supervisor's number. "I'm calling to brief him on our status."

Sergeant Wright answered on the first ring. "I'm glad you finally checked in. We've got units on the way to Lake Marie as we speak. Officers are about ten minutes out. Are you and Liz okay? Were you hurt in the explosion?"

"We're safe. For now. We're at the neighbors' house." He moved to the edge of a window and peeked out. "Looks like the remnants of the hit team moved out once the firefighters arrived."

"I can arrange something else if you think you're in danger."

Oz considered requesting separate hotel rooms with a locked door between them but decided against the notion.

"I believe we're okay, and we both could use some

rest." He glanced across the room at Liz, who had curled up on the couch with a blanket, her eyes already closed.

"We got the call logs back from the burner phone Liz gave Tillie before she was killed and traced the number of the person who called minutes before her time of death. Looks like his name is Milton Herzer. They lived in a halfway house together for several months. He's still there."

Oz grabbed a pen and notepad from the counter. "Great. Any matches on the shoe prints?"

"Nothing yet other than a size ten."

A task was exactly what Oz needed. They could stay put for the rest of the day and get some much-needed sleep at opposite ends of the house. Anything closer might be too tempting, and he wasn't sure they could resist their attraction again. Work was their only option, even if being out in public was a bit risky. Staying here alone was even riskier.

"Give me the address. We'll head that way first thing in the morning."

Serenity Cove sat nestled in the Smoky Mountains about five miles from the lake house and backed up to national parklands. The sun rose over the mountains, and Oz sipped a fresh cup of coffee while driving the precinct's unmarked SUV down a gravel road lined with evergreen trees.

He'd always wanted a place like this. Acres of pastureland tucked back off the main road with a large creek that ran alongside the mile-long drive. Horses dotted the landscape, and two dogs barked from the black split-rail fence line marking the perimeter of the owner's land.

They pulled in front of a two-story log home where a couple of red rocking chairs and a hammock designed for a lazy afternoon nap decorated the covered front porch.

Liz sat next to him and seemed rested after their uneventful night at the neighbors' cabin. She must've slept like a baby. Oz, on the other hand, dreamed about their kiss all night and struggled to give his mind a much-needed break.

She leaned forward and looked out the windshield. "Wow. This place is amazing. Are you sure this is a halfway house?"

"According to the address Sarge gave me. He said they run all kinds of therapy programs to help people overcome addiction. Milton Herzer completed his court-ordered rehab a year ago and was hired to work with their equestrian program. Seems he has a knack with horses."

The slam of a screen door sounded next to them, and a woman with gray hair underneath her cowboy hat and a friendly smile stepped from the porch. "Can I help y'all?"

Oz rolled down his window and flashed his badge. "We're looking for Milton Herzer. Can you tell us where we can find him?"

"Sure." She pointed down the road. "If you head south for about a mile, you'll come to some train tracks. Cross those and then the barn is about half a mile up the hill. Milton's usually there or somewhere close by."

They headed in the direction the woman suggested and wound through the gorgeous acreage without much conversation. Earlier, when they'd stopped for a quick breakfast, neither of them brought up the kiss from last night. In some ways, he was thankful Liz didn't want to hash out what happened between them, but then again, she *had* been the one to stop things cold.

"Do you still talk to your brother?" She shifted in her seat toward him.

"Not since the day I testified against him."

Oz didn't like talking about his brother or his wife's death. Maybe that was the problem—the reason why after five years he still hadn't moved on with someone else.

"What about your parents? Do they visit him?"

"After the trial they moved out west. They still call on my birthday but after Clay went to jail our family wasn't the same."

A lone train whistle blew in the distance. The crossing beam lowered in front of the tracks, and Oz slowed the SUV to a stop.

"Since Roni died, I've not really had anyone in my life other than my colleagues at work."

A railroad trestle bridge crossed the river a hundred yards on their left, and from the right, deep in the woods, one bright headlight approached their position. He glanced at Liz who watched the train.

"I can't even imagine. Losing your family like that with one horrific tragedy. Must've been awful."

"Still is."

The whistle blew again—the perfect mournful sound to the topic at hand. He missed his wife. And his brother. He'd been close to Clay growing up, but his brother changed during his teens and his betrayal was too deep for Oz to overcome. Only by the grace of God had he been able to forgive and not hate his brother for his actions. The best thing for Clay now was to sober up while on the inside.

Liz reached over and wrapped her fingers around his hand. "I want you to know that no matter what happens during this case, I don't regret our kiss."

Neither did he. That was the problem, but she'd been clear, and he wasn't one to cross any lines. "I guess we can chalk that up to poor judgment and exhaustion."

His resolve to remain professional weakened with her touch and he placed his hand back on the wheel as a loud engine revved behind them.

Bright headlights glared through the rearview mirror and barreled toward their SUV, not slowing down for the crossing. Oz shifted into Drive but was too late.

The large truck slammed into the rear of their car. Metal crunched and flung his body into the steering wheel. The rear compartment crushed into the back seat. He hit the brakes with both feet. Tires squealed. Smoke boiled around them, limiting his visibility. Brute force from the truck pushed them onto the tracks. The train gained ground toward the crossing and blared the horn as a warning.

The truck backed off, leaving them stranded. Oz turned the key in the ignition, but the car wouldn't start. He tried again. With each attempt, the train sped closer.

"Get out." Oz unbuckled his belt. "The car won't crank. There's a fuel safety switch that cuts the gas to the engine in the case of an accident, and I don't have time to reset it."

Liz grabbed her seat belt and tugged. "It's stuck."

He pressed the release and pulled. No movement. The train blew its horn again, an alarm to the inevitable collision. White steam billowed closer, and Oz jerked the shoulder strap hoping he could tear it loose from the side.

The red engine barreled forward, and air brakes squealed their effort to stop, but with all the weighted cars pushing the locomotive down the tracks, the engineer would never be able to avoid impact.

If they didn't get out now, they'd both die.

SIX

Liz grabbed her key ring and selected the knife blade she kept attached—a present from her father when she started driving at sixteen. If she didn't hurry, she'd never see him again. The thought almost made her sick, and she pushed the notion aside, working faster to get out while she could.

With her thumb, she pressed the slider up and sliced the blade across the shoulder and waist strap. Her fingers fumbled for the handle, and she leaned into the door with the weight of her shoulder, tumbling onto the crossties. Vibrations from the moving train pulsated against her palms, growing stronger with every second.

Cold wind rushed against her face, and iron wheels clacked an eerie rhythm as the long freight train barreled in her direction.

The engineer waved his hand out the side window in an effort to clear the tracks and then blared the train horn again.

She raced to the front of the car, grabbed Oz's hand and leaped across to safety just in time. They rolled to the ground on the other side and Liz looked back. The train sped forward, crashing into the car. Metallic sparks

Enjoying Your Book?

Start saving on new books like the one you're reading with the *Harlequin Reader Service!*

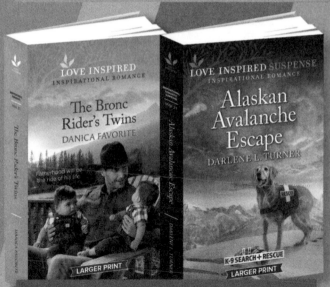

Get Free Books In Just 3 Easy Steps

Are you an avid reader searching for more books?
The **Harlequin Reader Service** might be for you! We'd love to send
you up to **4 free books** just for trying it out. Just write **"YES"** on the
Free Books Voucher Card and we'll send your free books and a gift,
altogether worth over $20.

Step 1: Choose your Books

Try *Love Inspired*® Romance Larger-Print and get 2 books and fall in
love with inspirational romances that take you on an uplifting journey
of faith, forgiveness and hope.

Try *Love Inspired*® Suspense Larger-Print and get 2 books where
courage and optimism unite in stories of faith and love in the face of
danger.

Or *TRY BOTH!*

Step 2: Return your completed Free Books Voucher Card

Step 3: Receive your books and continue reading!

Your free books are **completely free**, even the shipping! If you continue
with your subscription, you can look forward to curated monthly
shipments of brand-new books from your selected series, always at a
discount off the cover price! Plus you can cancel any time.

Don't miss out, reply today! Over $20 FREE value.

Free Books Voucher Card

YES! I love reading, please send me more books from the series I'd like to explore and a free gift from each series I select.

More books are just 3 steps away!

Just write in "**YES**" on the dotted line below then select your series and return this Books Voucher today and we'll send your free books & a gift asap!

▶▶ *YES* ◀◀

Choose your books:

☐ **Love Inspired®**
Romance
Larger-Print
122/322 CTI G29D

☐ **Love Inspired®**
Suspense
Larger-Print
107/307 CTI G29D

☐ **BOTH**
122/322 & 107/307
CTI G29F

FIRST NAME   LAST NAME

ADDRESS

APT.#   CITY

STATE/PROV.   ZIP/POSTAL CODE

EMAIL ☐ Please check this box if you would like to receive newsletters and promotional emails from Harlequin Enterprises ULC and its affiliates. You can unsubscribe anytime.

LI/LIS-1123-OM_123ST

BUSINESS REPLY MAIL
FIRST-CLASS MAIL   PERMIT NO. 717   BUFFALO, NY

POSTAGE WILL BE PAID BY ADDRESSEE

HARLEQUIN READER SERVICE
PO BOX 1341
BUFFALO NY 14240-8571

NO POSTAGE
NECESSARY
IF MAILED
IN THE
UNITED STATES

flew into the air upon impact. A few seconds longer and she would've been dead. The force of the hit alone would've killed her instantly, but thanks to dear old Dad and the grace of God, she was alive.

The cold asphalt seeped through the fabric of her pants as the train continued to scrape down the tracks. Heavy weighted boxcars pushed the engine forward. Debris littered the area around them, and Liz covered her head. Dirt and pieces pelted her back as she prayed for the engineer driving the train or any other workers inside. *Please God. Keep them safe.*

When the cars stopped moving, she ran to the front and tried to see inside. An older gentleman stepped down from the compartment, black soot on his face, dressed in gray coveralls and a ball cap. Relief softened his wide eyes when he saw her. "Oh, thank goodness. I saw you jump but wasn't sure you got out of the way in time."

He wiped his forehead and left a red smudge from a small cut near his brow. "Are y'all okay?"

"We're fine. How about you?"

"I think so. I hit my head with the impact, but it ain't nothin' more than a scratch. I tried everything I knew to stop Ole Bess, but when she's loaded this heavy, it takes a while. The best part of the track is about two miles back that way, and we love to open her up. We slow a bit for the crossings, but sometimes these freighters take at least a mile to come to a complete halt. Wasn't expecting anyone to be on the tracks when we came around the bend."

"This wasn't your fault. We were pushed onto the tracks, and the SUV wouldn't start."

"What do you mean *pushed*?" The old man looked behind her.

Oz tugged her arm. "We've gotta go. They're coming up both sides."

Men dressed in black ran next to the tracks. The large ballast stones along the edges slowed them down, but she wasn't sure they could outrun them. "How many cars are on this train?"

"About ninety."

Liz pointed to the ladder on the side. "What if we climb to the top and cross the cars until we're in the clear?"

The engineer shook his head. "The gaps between the boxcars are too wide and will be hard to jump. If you climb up and then down for each car, these guys will catch up to you in no time. All they'd have to do is wait for you to come to them." He turned and pointed toward the bridge in front of the train. "Your best chance is to cross the trestle up ahead. There's a small town about half a mile on the other side."

Oz pulled his weapon. "Or I can try to hold them off."

"We don't have enough ammunition. Not without backup, and I don't want to put this man in any danger. I say we take the bridge."

"The trestle it is, but if we're going to make it, then we need to go now."

She took off running toward the curvature of the track while Oz stayed behind firing off several rounds to keep their attackers at a distance. Once she reached the end, she ducked behind a tree and scanned the landscape in front of her.

Red lights up ahead indicated the next crossing at the small town the engineer mentioned. They wouldn't have to go far if they could keep their assailants at bay. The large railroad trestle rose amongst the trees, about fifty feet away, covering Lake Marie below.

Oz raced to her location and flattened against a tree next to her. "I'm out of ammunition. Do you have an extra magazine?"

She pulled one from her pocket and handed it to him. "It's only nine rounds, and the only way to the town is across that."

His face paled when he looked at the trestle. "I thought the beams were closer together."

"We'll need to walk across, then head into town, find the police station or some cell service to call Sergeant Wright and direct backup officers to our location."

With another peek back toward the trainwreck, she motioned toward the bridge. "Time to move. They're gaining ground."

Liz led the way and reached the trestle first. She placed her boot on one crosstie at a time, trying not to slip. Dark water rippled beneath her and slapped the shoreline. The distance to the surface was no more than thirty feet. If this were a hot summer day instead of the middle of winter, she'd jump into the lake below for a refreshing swim like she used to do when she was a kid. She knew all the good jumping rocks and rope swings on her dad's lake. Many of them were much higher than this, but this was the first time she had crossed a train trestle before.

Cold wind blew, and her eyes teared. She swiped a hand across the moisture and kept moving to the middle of the bridge. Oz lagged behind a bit.

"Hurry or we won't make it," she said.

"It's high."

"Not really. I've jumped off higher when I was a kid."

Oz didn't respond and still stood at the first beam,

staring at the water below. Liz walked back toward him. "Please tell me you're not afraid of heights?"

"Okay. I won't tell you."

"Look at me. This is our only way out of here. You have to take the first step."

She wrapped his hand in hers and pulled him forward. He'd saved her life multiple times lately, and this was her chance to help him.

Oz slid his foot forward and clasped the vertical iron beams supporting the metal archway covering the bridge, and she had to tug at him to release his grip until the next one. The lateral edge was only a step or two away, and a cloud of fog floated above the surface, providing a few glimpses of the dark green water underneath.

"We're halfway there. Keep moving."

Boots slapped the other end of the bridge. Multiple armed men emerged from the shadows and blocked their path. Liz released Oz's hand and pulled her weapon. So much for their escape plan.

From the pale shade of Oz's face, the last place he wanted to be stuck was a train trestle high in the air. There was only one way off this bridge. Down. He wasn't going to be happy.

"We've got a problem." She raised her gun.

One of the men stepped forward, a black knit cap on his head and red stubble grazing his jawline. She recognized him—Clive Hawkins, the leader of the East Mountain Mafia and Tillie's former crush.

"You're a hard woman to track down." He spat on the ground and held out his tattooed arms as if he were welcoming her to the dark side. "But we finally found you."

Liz looked behind Oz. The other members had reached

them and blocked their retreat. Oz stared at the water below but kept his weapon aimed at the group behind them, who appeared to be waiting for their leader's instructions before moving closer.

She turned back to Clive, who took another step forward. "How'd you get past us and to the other side so fast?"

"We split into groups. A couple of us covered the train while the rest made our way to the next town up. No matter your direction, we were ready. From the looks of things, you've really got nowhere to go except with us."

She turned and leaned toward Oz, keeping her voice low. "We're gonna have to jump."

"I don't think so. It's too high."

"It's the only way."

He lifted his gaze from the water and met hers. "I can't."

"We don't have a choice. You can swim, right?"

He looked back down and stared at the water below. "Yeah, but maybe we can negotiate with them. Get them to let us walk."

Liz glanced over his shoulder at the gang blocking their retreat. "I doubt it. They look determined to leave with what they came for, and I'm not willing to give them that without a fight."

Lines creased Oz's forehead, and his complexion paled, his body frozen with fear. "Move with me," she said. "Small steps. We need to be closer to the edge."

"Detective, you might as well stop trying to figure out a way to get by us with your partner and surrender. We're not here to hurt you."

She ignored Clive's remarks and leaned closer to Oz. "We can do this."

He shook his head. "The water is freezing this time

of year. We'll have hypothermia before we get to the bank."

"No, we won't. It's a power plant lake. The water filters through and cools their turbines, which makes the water warmer than a natural lake. That's why there's fog above the surface. Gotta be at least seventy-five degrees. We'll still be cold, but we won't freeze. At least not until we get out."

Liv stepped closer to the edge. Oz moved with her. Slanted steel beams supported the bridge from the top of the arch to the tracks but left wide openings for both of them.

"You might as well put your guns away," Clive said. "I'd hate for anybody to get hurt."

"Like you hurt Tillie?" Liz aimed her weapon in the man's direction and squeezed Oz's hand with the other.

"I have no idea what you're talking about."

"Tillie Blue. Young woman. Nineteen. Pretty. She was killed recently in her apartment, and you were the hired hit man."

"That's quite an accusation, Detective, and completely false. I've been out of town the past couple of days."

"I don't believe you. You were there, in her apartment, shot her and then attacked me. I'm guessing you didn't kill me then because I wasn't your mark, and the East Mountain Mafia never does anything without a payment, but someone's paying you now, aren't they?"

The smug look on his face tightened as he took another step. She still had no memory of the murder, but pretending like she did might provide a lead. Clive didn't take the bait.

"They want to talk to you," he said. "Come with us and we'll let your friend go, unharmed."

"*They* want to kill me so the evidence about Tillie's murder never sees the light of day."

"If that were the case then you'd be dead. We have resources well beyond anything even I could imagine. Best thing for you is to come with us. We'll go for a little drive, drop your friend off in town and take you to the designated location."

Anxiety tightened the muscles in her chest. "And where would that be? A watery grave down by the river? No, thanks."

The East Mountain Mafia had a way of making their enemies disappear without ever finding the bodies. There was a whole bulletin board full of missing person reports related to their activities, and none of them had ever been found. She wasn't about to become a flyer on the wall.

"Who wants to see me? Give me a name."

He motioned toward the crash site. "I don't think you're in a position to make demands. Let's not make this harder than it needs to be."

Liz scanned the water for boats. The surface was clear. Not surprising since most of the homes were zoned as vacation properties and only active during the summer months.

"Not trying to make things hard. I just want a name."

She stalled for time to give Oz a moment to prepare for the inevitable plunge and to get Clive to talk. He hadn't denied being in Tillie's apartment, but from the smirk on his face, he wasn't going to offer up a confession in the middle of a bridge when she had no leverage and was surrounded by armed gunmen. Someone with money and power was funding EMM services, but he'd never give her a name when he had the upper hand.

"Can't do that." He took another step.

"Stay where you are. Like you said, I don't want anyone to get hurt either."

Oz squeezed her hand.

"Are you ready?" she whispered. No reply.

Clive raised his palm in the air. "No need for weapons, Detective. I promise we won't hurt you. We were paid to keep you alive."

"And who in this town would do that? I'm new and came here as a cop. No one really knows me because I spend most of my time at work and have few friends."

"You have at least one who wants to keep you safe. That's why we're here."

"Then why did you push us onto the train tracks?"

"We didn't. That was someone else."

With one flick of Clive's wrist, his black-suited gang marched across the bridge from both ends, advancing faster with their guns raised.

Liz squeezed Oz's hand. "Now."

She leaped from the side with him in tow. His wife's red scarf snagged on the beam and pulled away, left to dangle from the bridge. Nerves rose to her throat and wind rushed against her ears. The fall was long and fast with nothing but the lake awaiting their plunge.

She closed her eyes and held her breath. Warm water slapped her body as the surface tension broke and swallowed her into the depths, tearing Oz's hand away. Muffled shouts echoed from above as she sank into the black abyss, alone.

His lungs burned for oxygen, but Oz reached for Liz instead. Sunlight-streaked water helped his search, but not even a shadow floated by. The force of their landing pulled them apart, and the more he groped the farther he sank from the surface. He kicked to the top, inhaled a gulp of air, then dove back down.

Still no Liz.

He swam farther down, hoping for any ripple or sign of life, and even though the fog had burned off, he came up empty. Cold wind chilled his face, but he kept searching. Liz had to be a strong swimmer, spending her childhood summers at the lake. Maybe she made the distance to shore.

Above him, Clive shouted commands, and truck engines roared to life. Oz wished he could've seen the look on the man's face when they jumped. The EMM leader had lost his mark again and was not the kind of person to accept failure well. The trucks moved off-road, through the trees and down the bank toward the shoreline. If Oz didn't find Liz soon, then Clive and his gang might not be unsuccessful, after all.

Water erupted to his left in a small hidden cove. Sunlight highlighted Liz's pale face, and she remained against the tree line out of sight of Clive's trucks. Oz swam toward her, never so happy to see someone in all his life.

"Thank goodness. I thought you drowned." Oz reached out, took her hand and pulled her back into the shadows of the cove.

"I lost your wife's scarf. It's still on the bridge. Maybe we can go back—"

"The last thing I'm worried about right now is a scarf. We've gotta move. Clive is headed down here and will see us when he rounds that bend. Can you swim to the marina? It's just inside that cove over there."

"Of course."

The Lake Marie Marina housed hundreds of boats,

especially during the winter months, and provided plenty of places to hide. He hoped one of the owner's left their door unlocked so they could slip inside out of the frigid temperatures.

"Do you still have your phone?"

"In the waterproof case."

"They'll have cell service, and I can call the precinct from there. Have them redirect our backup to our location and arrest these guys. Maybe then we can find out who's behind all of this."

"I'm still confused why they didn't shoot me. He said they were paid to keep me alive. He has to be lying, right?"

"I've heard and seen stranger things."

Truck engines revved closer, and a cloud of dust rose into the air one cove over. "Time to go."

They sank beneath the surface of the water and swam away from the lower dirt road circling the perimeter of the lake. Liz remained submerged almost the entire distance, but he had to surface twice before reaching the marina. All the boats, lined up in the slips, would provide cover as long as Clive and his gang stayed in their trucks.

The marina held a large number of small luxury cabin cruisers with living accommodations beneath the main deck. Several houseboats also bobbed in sequence and overshadowed the smaller pontoons and V hulls moored in between. One sailboat's mast rose into the sky but the Dacron material had seen better days.

"Do you want to get out?" Oz swam down one of the aisles to avoid being spotted. Clive and his caravan had disappeared out of sight, but the road circled back at the end. Maybe they'd give up and go home. But maybe they wouldn't. Now was the time to find a good hiding place until backup arrived.

"The air's cold even with the sun high in the sky." She held on to the side of one of the docks. "And I'm tired of being cold. Let's pick out one of these house-boats and get inside. We can turn on the heat, call for re-inforcements and if we're lucky, find something to eat."

"How about that one?" Oz pointed to a sleek black luxury houseboat. "Might as well make the most of our situation." He swam over to the patio ladder someone forgot to stow upon leaving.

Liz followed. "You would pick the newer one most likely outfitted with a top-of-the-line security system. Cameras and alarms will alert the owner we're here."

"Already has." An elderly man with white hair and fierce blue eyes stood over them with a pistol pointed at their heads.

"You two need to back away from my boat. I don't take to kindly to stowaways."

Oz lifted his badge to the surface. "Sir, we work for the Mills Creek Police Department, and we'd like for you to reconsider."

The man slipped on his glasses hanging from a neck chain and inspected the badge. He tucked his gun back into his holster. "Come on up."

Once inside, the man handed them both a bath towel and motioned to a gas stove already warming the room. "Wanna tell me why two detectives are swimming around a marina in the freezing cold weather?"

"Would you believe for a case?" Oz asked.

The old man pointed to a framed police certificate on his wooden mantle. "I would."

He extended his hand. "Hank Butler, retired captain

with the NYPD. I've done some crazy things when I worked as a detective. Although I don't think I went swimming in a lake in the middle of December."

Liz raised her palms to the flames. "How'd you end up in North Carolina?"

"My sweet Norma and I used to vacation down here in the summers, God rest her soul. She loved this place and would beg me to transfer, but I was too stubborn about my career back then. Once our kids were grown, they all moved to warmer lower-taxed states, so when I retired, we decided to do the same. I gave my sweet wife the life she always wanted. My only regret is I should've done it sooner. She passed away three years after moving here."

"I'm so sorry," Liz said.

"Nothing to be sorry about. Death is part of life, and she's in a much better place now. Some days I just wish I could be with her."

"This certainly is a gorgeous boat. Looks brand new," Oz said.

"Bought her last year. Our first houseboat was the one next to us, which my best friend bought after Norma passed. I couldn't bear to stay there, and I bought this beauty instead. Got a good deal I couldn't pass up."

Oz held up the phone. "I don't want to be rude, but I need to text my sergeant, if that's okay."

"Go ahead." Hank pointed at Liz. "Would you like some hot coffee? It's fresh."

"I would."

"I'll pour you both a cup." He moved into the kitchen and pulled two mugs from the open shelf.

Liz leaned closer to Oz. "I don't want Clive and the

EMM to find us here where there could be a civilian casualty."

"I thought of that too. One cup of coffee and then we find a vacated boat until backup arrives."

Hank crossed the room and handed them their steaming cups. "Did I hear you mention the East Mountain Mafia? I read about their criminal activity in the paper all the time."

The man had good hearing for his age.

"I did, so we don't plan to stay here. We'll finish our coffee and move to a different spot so you won't be in any danger. Although you might want to stay inside and away from windows until more units arrive."

"Don't be absurd. I worked on the gang unit for years. We can take them."

Liz wrapped her fingers a bit tighter around the mug and admired his fortitude. "We don't want a gunfight. One, because we're outnumbered, and two, we're low on ammunition."

"Then we hide you. The boat I mentioned earlier, the one my best friend purchased, is moored right beside me. He's been sick for about a year, in and out of hospitals, and is staying with his daughter now until he gets stronger. As for the boat, no one's been inside for a while, but you can hide there. The interior lacks a bit, but I doubt they will even think to look there because the boat's outside appearance is even worse."

Oz gulped down the last of the coffee. "Sounds perfect. If anyone comes to your door, don't talk to them. Might be best if they think no one's home."

"Don't worry about me. If they stop by, I'll send them in the opposite direction, and if that doesn't work, I've always got Ole Stanley."

He motioned to the sawed-off shotgun leaned against the wall within arm's reach of the door. The hum of a distant boat echoed across the lake and Oz moved to the window. A Mastercraft Prostar moved at a high rate of speed toward the marina. Two more followed.

The man stepped up next to him and peered over his shoulder. "I take it that's your friends? Sure do have good taste in boats."

"Probably stole them." Oz let the curtain fall back into place and hit Send on the quick text to his sergeant for backup. He prayed the message went through. "We need to go ahead and move to your friend's boat. I don't want you to be caught in the middle of this. These men are armed and dangerous. Could be a gunfight."

"Not if I go with them." Liz placed her mug on the counter.

"We're not handing you over to them." Oz turned back to Hank. "Which way do we go?"

"Follow me."

They trailed the man down a narrow hallway to the back of the cabin, then climbed across to a small patio area. Oz helped Liz and then checked the sliding glass door. "Locked."

"I've got a key." The old man rummaged through a nearby drawer. "Found it." He stepped across and unlatched the entrance. "Move quickly. Their engines have stopped, and they'll be on the gangplanks soon."

Oz stepped inside. The friend's boat was the opposite of luxury. More like a tin can out of the '70s. Large colored bulbs hung along the edge of the ceiling, and a ratty hammock swung toward the paneled wall.

"Thanks for all your help. I apologize for the inconvenience," Oz said.

"What else have I got to do during the winter? Now get inside and hide." Hank pulled the adjoining plank back to his boat and disappeared inside his cabin.

Oz locked the door and peeked out its diamond-shaped window. The boardwalk was empty for the moment. He walked down the hallway to the main living area and kitchen combined.

Foul odors reeked of fishy live wells and forgotten food items souring in the fridge. Green carpet stretched the entire length of the room with orange furniture flanking the dark paneled walls.

The interior lacked windows and was void of natural light except for the patio door. On any other occasion, Oz would've bolted, but they needed cover, and the old man was right. No one would ever expect to find them inside this hunk of junk.

The dimly lit setting provided a good hiding place from Clive's gang. The men were close, as their shouts echoed across the water. Beams of light panned through neighboring boats and flashed through several windows at the stern. "They're looking inside. Get down."

Oz pulled her arm, and she toppled next to him into a small dark corner. Her hair dripped on his pants, and she pulled her cold hand from his. He grabbed a not-so-fresh blanket from the chair next to him, pulled the cover over their heads and Liz closer. Her body shook against him.

"The blanket smells like a wet dog."

"Yeah, well…this wet dog is determined to keep them from finding us."

Footsteps thumped across the platforms sandwiched between each boat. Light beamed through the neighboring craft and swept the interior. He heard the old man's voice. "Can I help you, gentlemen?"

"Have you seen a woman and man in the area? We're bounty hunters and need to bring this couple in. They skipped their bail hearing."

"Interesting, and yeah, I saw them. They headed past my boat and on up the hill to the restaurant there. Must've been hungry 'cause they seemed to be in a hurry."

"Thanks. We'll check once we finish down here."

"Okay, but seems like a waste of time to me, checking all these boats." The old man kept them talking to buy them some time.

"We're next. They'll know this blanket isn't right." Liz pushed up from the floor. "We need to find a better hiding place."

She scanned the room. "How about underneath the banquette? The angle of the windows won't allow them a viewpoint."

"You mean where all the rat droppings are?"

"It's the only blind spot."

They didn't have time to argue, and he grabbed her hand, then pulled her into the cramped space, positioning Liz in front of him. They ducked their heads, curled together into a fetal position and covered their bodies with the blanket. A beam of light brushed across the shag carpet coming within inches of their spot.

He tugged her a bit closer and wrapped his hands over hers, trying to warm her up. They both needed dry clothes and some hot soup, but until the threat moved away, they remained in place. He leaned close to her ear. "Are you okay?"

"I'm lying in rat poop, so no, I'm not okay."

Once the light beam moved to another section of

the dock, she pulled free from his arms and went back to the carpeted section, wrapping the blanket around her again. "Do you think it's safe to head back to the old man's place? I could use another cup of coffee and maybe a hot shower if he doesn't mind."

"Not yet." Oz peered through one of the side windows. "They're still searching."

She tucked her knees to her chest, her body continuing to shiver. "Clive said someone wanted to talk to me. Who do you think that is?"

"Someone who has enough money to hire the East Mountain Mafia." Oz walked through the cabin, remaining in the shadows, and found a thermostat. "Are they far enough away so they won't hear a furnace kick on?"

Liz looked out the window. "Yeah. They're headed up the hill now, toward the restaurant. Once they go inside, they can't see us." She plopped onto the couch. "He said they weren't hired to kill me. Don't you find that odd?"

"I think he's a liar and don't believe anything he says."

"He knows Tillie."

"And probably Tillie's father."

"Jeremiah does tend to have some questionable friends."

Oz bumped the furnace up to eighty, and the device hummed to life, warming the room. "That stinks." Liz covered her nose and mouth.

"Like something crawled into the ducts and died, but we need the heat." He took a seat beside her as sirens sounded in the distance. "Not much longer. Help is on the way."

A stampede of footsteps ran down the main boardwalk. Oz moved to a small kitchen window and looked out. Men in black jumped into speedboats tied to the platform, one slip over from their location.

"A few sirens and they all run for cover. Not so brave now, are they?" Liz stepped toward the patio door. An outside glow bounced into the room and highlighted her face. She froze in place. "Oz?"

He turned toward the patio doors.

Clive stood on the other side of the glass, holding the flashlight, and stared into the old houseboat. Not the man they wanted to see.

SEVEN

Oz bolted across the room for Liz, but he was too late. With one smooth jump onto the patio, Clive burst through the door, grabbed Liz and pulled her outside. Oz followed, but a strong body slammed him from the right and grappled him into a choke hold.

His police training kicked in and he landed several blows but his assailant matched his abilities, unwilling to surrender. He couldn't help Liz until he took this guy out. Oz maneuvered around the man, wrestled him into a secure hold and flipped him onto his stomach. He pressed all his strength onto his torso and pinned the man to the ground, landing several punches, but he kept squirming. Liz clung to a handrail as Clive tried to pull her free.

"Fight," Oz said, unable to help her.

Liz kicked her foot into Clive's knee. He stumbled backward, released his hold and ran with a limp for the last boat ready to pull out. Oz tightened his grip on the criminal he'd secured and held his clasped hands behind his back.

Blue lights reflected off the water, and the familiar barking of a K-9 unit echoed from the bank. Several officers raced after the gang members, but the boats took off at full speed.

One of the officers tossed Oz a pair of handcuffs, helped hoist the criminal to his feet and led him off to a squad car.

"You two sure know how to get into trouble," Bronson said when they joined him on the dock.

Liz motioned toward the disappearing boat lights. "The rest of them are headed south. Once they make it to their trucks, they'll use the back roads to get away."

Bronson squeezed his radio and issued a BOLO for the vehicles. "Headed south on Road 34 from the marina toward the Lake End Restaurant. Get a couple of units there ASAP."

He turned back to Oz and Liz, then nodded to the boat behind them. "Any idea who he is?"

Hank stood on his second-level patio and raised a glass. "Great work. Thanks for the entertainment. I've not seen that much excitement since I left the streets of New York City."

With a quick wave, Oz turned back to Bronson. "He's a retired police captain who helped us earlier."

Bronson motioned toward the steep incline at the end of the dock. "I've got a car heated and ready to take you to the precinct. Also, Sergeant Wright has arranged to put both of you up at the hotel with guards." His partner led the way up the hill. "Admin is working on the logistics."

"Thanks, but I'm done hiding out," Liz said. "I'll be staying in my apartment tonight. You're welcome to place some guards there if you want."

"Then you'll need this." Bronson opened the driver's

door and pulled a weapon off his seat. "Sergeant Wright told me to give this back to you. Everything cleared."

"That's great." She pressed her police-issued 9mm into her jacket pocket. "Glad to have it back."

Oz stood next to the door. "You'll need it if you return to your apartment. Clive knows where you live, and he'll find you there."

"I don't care. If he shows up, then maybe I'll finally learn what's going on. Whoever hired him to find me must not want me dead because he's had plenty of opportunities to kill me, and I'm still alive."

"Maybe the person who hired him wants to be the one to give you the ax. If we're going to solve this case, then you of all people can't take risks."

Bronson stepped between the two of them. "I've got a better idea. Why don't we all go back to the precinct and I'll let you interrogate the guy who called Tillie a few minutes before she was shot."

"You found him?" Oz pulled off his wet jacket and tossed it on the front seat, then stood next to the door where heat radiated from the warm cab. "That's who we were headed to see before a large truck pushed our SUV onto the tracks."

"Yeah, we found him, but he's not being cooperative. At least not with our officers. I figured one of you might want to talk to him." Bronson dangled the keys in the air.

Liz grabbed them from his fingers and slid into the open driver's seat. "He's the reason Tillie's dead, and I want answers. I'm tired of playing defense." She glanced up at Oz. "You coming?"

"Right behind you."

"Good. 'Cause it's cold out there, and you're letting the heat out."

After driving for an hour, they arrived at the precinct. Oz walked to the break room and filled two hot cups of coffee—one for Liz, the other for him. They were pretty much dry from running the heater the entire way back to the department, but exhaustion from their adrenaline crash took hold. Caffeine was the only thing able to clear his mind and keep him awake while interrogating Tillie's caller.

He handed Liz a mug decorated with a pair of handcuffs on the side with three words underneath—*strong*, *trustworthy* and *protector*. A good description of the woman standing in front of him. "You ready?"

"Absolutely. You?"

He smiled, stepped across the hall and opened the interrogation room door. "Never better."

"Wait." Sergeant Wright walked toward them, his phone in hand. "Liz, I want you to do the interview alone."

Oz closed the door and kept his hand on the knob. "But this is a homicide case. She's Narcotics."

"I know, but this man is a former dealer and still has ties to the cartel. They're a different breed than a random criminal. They won't talk unless they have a bit of trust in the other person, and since she knows him, she's the best one to do the interrogation."

Wright handed Liz a folder. She flipped open the cover and scrolled through the images and documents. "Our investigators found some pertinent information when they searched his apartment. Should help you to get him to talk."

"You said that I know him?" Liz asked.

"Yeah. You met him during the Vista sting while undercover. They call him Greasy Lee otherwise known as Milton Lee Herzer. Ring a bell?"

"Didn't he help us with that operation when I first came on board? What's he doing joining the EMM?"

"Not sure he has, although he definitely has ties to the group and he's the only person we have connecting Tillie to them."

"Won't that blow Liz's cover for future stings, if he sees her outside of her role?" Oz peered through the small square window at the man. Long black hair slicked back on his head into a low ponytail. Couldn't be more than two hundred pounds.

"She already has a rapport, and he knows she's a cop." Sergeant Wright motioned to the observation room. "We'll be in there."

Oz liked to interrogate his own criminals, especially when they were tied to his cases, but when his sergeant insisted, he had no other choice but to oblige.

They took their places as Liz entered the room separated from them by two-way mirrored glass. "You should've let me do this," Oz said again.

Wright pulled out a stool and took a seat. "I forget this is the first time you've worked with her. Don't underestimate Detective Burke. She's got far more fortitude than most."

"She's definitely a risk-taker, but I'm not sure I'd call that fortitude."

His sergeant smiled. "Would you have jumped off the bridge had she not been there? Because if not, you'd probably be dead right now. If that's not fortitude, then I don't know what is."

Oz leaned back against the wall. The man was right. Liz had saved his life today, and here he was airing his frustration about the interrogation when he should be supporting her.

Liz unloaded a series of targeted questions in a style that put the suspect at ease. Once the man started talking, she leaned back in her chair and prompted him only when the discussion began to slow. Her interrogation skills impressed Oz.

"We know you called her, Lee." Her voice rang through the intercom inside the room. "Only a few minutes before someone broke into her apartment, shot her in the head and then proceeded to attack me upon return. I told her not to open the door to anybody, so why do you think she did, unless it was someone she knew? Like you."

The man raised his palms to her. "I promise it wasn't me. I'd never hurt Tillie."

Liz pushed a photo of Tillie's lifeless body across the table. Oz smiled at her impeccable timing.

"Then who did this to her? If you're her friend, then help us find who *did* hurt her."

Greasy Lee shifted in his seat. "She told me not to talk about anything we discussed. Made me promise."

"And now she's dead. Do you want to be next? If this killer finds out you've been talking to us, then he won't stop until there's a bullet in your head too."

The man stared at the photo, then pushed the image back toward her. "I don't know any names. All I can tell you is that she had a boyfriend. Someone older."

Oz stepped closer to the window. "Come on, Liz. Don't let him get away with that. He knows who the man is."

Sergeant Wright stood and crossed to the door. "She won't. You'll see."

He left Oz in the room alone to watch Liz work. She stood from her chair and paced a few steps. "Did you ever see this man? A photo of him?"

"Nope. She never gave me any identifying information or showed me any pictures."

"Yet, you were one of her best friends. Were you jealous?"

The man sat back in his chair. "Of course not. We weren't like that."

Liz pulled out another photo of the blue sapphire ring Oz had noticed on Tillie's lifeless hand. Jewelry like that went for thousands of dollars, which Tillie didn't have, not as a recovering addict.

"Then why'd you buy this ring for her?"

He pulled the picture closer. "I didn't."

She placed a bagged receipt in front of him. "Officers found this in one of your drawers after they arrested you and searched your apartment. These are from Forester's Jewelers. Guess what listed item was purchased from there?" She paused for effect. "Time to come clean, Lee."

"I didn't buy it for her. He did, but she wouldn't tell me his name, so I swiped the receipts to try to figure out who this man was. Like you're doing now, Detective."

"I've had boyfriends before, but I've never gone through their drawers when I suspected them of questionable behavior. Sounds to me like you were more invested in Tillie than she was in you. How does it feel to know she loved someone other than you?"

Greasy Lee's neck turned red, and Liz kept coming at him. "Did you go to her apartment that night?"

"We only talked on the phone about random stuff."

"Did she tell you she was at home?"

"I figured she was. I could hear her dog barking in the background and the TV playing."

"Did anyone come to the door during your conversation?"

"Not that I recall."

Liz pulled Tillie's phone from the evidence bag and tapped the screen. She took her seat and passed the phone across to him.

"Come on, Lee. Don't lie to me. Tillie saved your text message. The one you left right after your call. You warned her about letting someone into the apartment." Liz picked up the phone and scrolled to the evidence. "In fact, your exact words were, *Don't let him in. He's not good for you.*"

Lee shifted in the chair and looked away from the screen.

"Give me a name." She folded her arms across her chest and leaned back against the wall, but he refused to answer. "I should arrest you right now."

"I'm not going back to jail."

"Then be honest with me. Help me find the person who did this to her." She tapped the photo of Tillie's dead body. "What happened that night?"

The swell of pride rose in Oz's chest. "Attagirl."

Greasy Lee pushed back from the table. "I don't have to take this. I'm innocent, and you don't have anything to hold me. I've told you everything I know."

"I do have enough to hold you. Officers found a suspicious little packet in your pocket. Enough to place you in jail for a few months at least." She took her seat. "Now tell me who Tillie was seeing."

"He's married, and that's all I know. I'm leaving."

He stepped toward the door, but Liz stood and moved in front of him, placing her hand against his chest.

"Take a seat, Greasy. We're not done here."

The man's eyes narrowed. He grabbed the chair and swung it at Liz, hitting her. She fell to the floor. Lee raised the chair over his head and hit her again.

Oz bolted from the observation room, swiped his access card and charged into the scene. The full force of Greasy Lee's body plowed into him, ready to take down anyone standing in his way of freedom.

Everything blurred around Liz, but she managed to push the chair to the side. Oz tumbled into the corner with Greasy Lee on top of him. He defended the blows, but at the moment her suspect had the upper hand. She had to help get him under control.

She moved to assist, using her body weight to help flip the man onto his stomach and cuff his hands. "Greasy Lee, you're under arrest for assaulting a police officer."

Two officers rushed in and muscled the suspect from the room, depositing Greasy Lee into a holding cell.

"Are you okay?" Oz faced her, ran a hand through his dark waves and leaned against the wall.

Pain throbbed through her head, and she touched the forming knot. "I'm not sure how much more my brain can take. You'd think by now someone would've knocked my memories back into place. Too bad I still can't recall my attacker in Tillie's apartment."

She stood and pushed the chair back under the table. "I'm mad at myself for not anticipating his attack. I should've seen that coming after provoking him. I'd hoped he would open up and tell me more."

"He knew he was in trouble and didn't want to go back to jail."

"Too late for that. I think he's afraid of more than prison. He's afraid of the person who killed Tillie. I just wish he would've told me more before he decided to lose it."

"We can always interrogate him again later." Oz stepped to the door. "Want some ibuprofen? I'm sure you have a headache."

"Yeah." She followed him to his desk. "At least we got one lead out of him."

"The married boyfriend Tillie was seeing? Who do you think that might be?"

"Not sure. Since she lied about her parents, I'm questioning everything she told me."

Tillie never mentioned any man in her life, especially a married one, but she and Lee were close. If anyone knew about her love life, he would. Oz opened his desk drawer and tossed Liz a bottle of ibuprofen. Bronson rounded the corner. "Sergeant wants to see you both in his office."

They wound their way through the detectives' work area past multiple cubicles and into an office with one large interior window. Sergeant Wright stood when they entered and motioned to a couple of chairs. "Well, you both look okay, and I watched the video but would like to hear the details. What happened in there?"

Liz launched into the scene, and Sergeant Wright listened without interruption. Oz jumped in here and there.

"Can you both make sure to file reports on this incident by end of day?"

"Of course," she said. "Actually, I'm glad you wanted

a briefing because there's something I would like to discuss with you."

"Go ahead."

"Sitting back and trying to hide me from the East Mountain Mafia is useless. We've had several run-ins now at safe houses, and they keep finding me. Clive mentioned someone wants to talk to me even though he wouldn't give us a name. I'm guessing they want to know how much I remember about Tillie's death. So I say we give them what they want. Let's give them me."

She kept her eyes on the sergeant, afraid to even look at Oz. He'd never agree since this was his case, and he worked hard to try to protect her, but she couldn't take the waiting one minute longer.

"I think this is a bad idea." Oz scooted to the edge of his seat and shifted his body toward her. "These men tried to kill you. The last thing we need to do is dangle you like bait."

"Running from them is not only putting me in danger but other officers as well. If we set up a meet, then we can control the security, the situation, without them knowing."

"A cop setting up a meeting? Trust me. They'll see that one coming a mile away," Oz said.

Sergeant Wright leaned back in his chair, pressed his fingertips together, and eyed Liz for a moment. "Approved. Write up the logistical plan and have it to me by end of day."

Oz stood. "It's too risky. She's the only witness we have to Tillie's murder. Without her, this case goes cold."

"A witness who can't remember. In most situations, I'd agree with you, Oz, but Detective Burke is well trained in undercover work. She's carried out multiple successful drug operations and been an integral part in dismantling their networks." He swiveled his leather chair to face Liz. "I'll take it to the captain and hopefully have the go ahead by tomorrow afternoon."

Liz gave him a small nod. "Thank you, sir. You won't be sorry."

"Before you go, I have some more news for you both."

Oz stopped at the door and waited while Sergeant Wright handed them a copy of a printed report. "We found the navy blue sedan."

She scanned the information he handed her. "Where?"

"In an abandoned lot at the edge of town. We brought it back to Impound, so if you want to take a look at the car, you can. I've already had our crime scene investigators go over it with a fine-tooth comb. Prints were wiped down, and there was no fabric, hairs or other identifying information for our killer."

"There are thousands of navy blue cars on the road. How do we know this is the one that was at Tillie's crime scene?" Oz asked.

Sergeant Wright swiveled his monitor for them to view. "Because the one thing we did find was a smear of Tillie's blood on the passenger seat. Probably transfer spatter from his clothes when he shot her."

Liz stared at the photo of the sedan as if the picture might bring back some memory from the incident. "Who's the car registered to?"

"It's part of a fleet service with a luxury line. The largest one in North Carolina. Thousands of people use these cars every day, and workers clean them in between customers."

"Which explains everything being wiped down." Liz took a seat again. "I'm surprised they missed the blood."

"We found a couple of smudges near the seat pull on the passenger side."

"Only wealthy types use a luxury fleet service—businessmen, government officials, corporate executives." Liz pointed at the screen again. "Have we subpoenaed their records or video footage?"

"We have, but due to Christmas being next week, I doubt we will get what we need until after the New Year."

In all the drama of her life, Liz had almost forgotten about the holidays. Her father was flying up from Florida to see her, and they were supposed to spend next week together. She hoped to have this case solved before he arrived. "Can you click on the image with the passenger door open?"

The sergeant did as she asked, and Oz stepped closer to the screen. "The seat's all the way back. Only a man would slide the seat back that far."

"Or a tall woman. I don't suppose they were able to grab any prints from the blood evidence," Liz said.

"'Fraid not."

She studied the image. Something about the car nagged at her. Maybe because it had been there the day of the murder, and even though she didn't remember, had she perhaps seen it out the window or something? "Can I keep a copy of that image?"

"I'll email them to you," Sarge said while sending the files.

"Thanks."

"Are we done here?" Oz moved to the door. "I've got work to do." He avoided her gaze. Probably still mad she'd gone over his head with the idea of an undercover operation. She wasn't trying to undermine his work, but she also wasn't going to be dismissed when she believed her idea would help the case.

Oz was cautious, and there was nothing wrong with his thoughtful work ethic. In some ways, she even admired his patience. She often wondered if the death of his wife cultivated his approach or if he'd always been careful with every case. Either way, she couldn't sit by any longer waiting for the next assault on her life. She had to take action.

Back at her desk, she pulled up a template and planned out the undercover logistics for the operation. She was about halfway into the details and still couldn't get the blue sedan out of her mind. She pulled up the images when a shadow fell across her desk, blocking the overhead fluorescent light. "Can I help you, Oz?"

"Please don't do this."

She rolled her chair around and looked up at his six-foot-three-inch frame propped against her cubicle. "I'm sorry, but I have to."

Liz understood his concern, especially with the trauma of his past, but she couldn't let her colleague's fear halt an operation to find Tillie's killer. Undercover work was her strength.

"You can't go up against the East Mountain Mafia. That's a death wish."

"If the EMM wanted me dead, I'd be dead." She turned to her screen. "It's not like I'll be alone. We'll put a team together and have plenty of backup when I meet with Clive. This may be the only way to find out who's behind all of this."

"The only way the money person will meet you is if you fake your memories because unless you've had some kind of miraculous recollection, you have nothing to give them. What happens when they figure out you don't remember anything?"

His logic annoyed her. "We know Clive was there and was likely our triggerman. What else do I need?" She pulled up Tillie's social media images. The more she knew about her CI's dealings before the murder the better. "Even you said Clive doesn't do anything without a payday, so we give him one. If he gives me the money-man, then he gets a lesser charge for pulling the trigger."

"Or we could bring him in. Interrogate him?"

"He won't talk. We've exhausted all our leads unless you have someone else in mind."

"What about Tillie's father, Jeremiah Foxx? I believe he's involved somehow."

Liz paused her scrolling. "Maybe so. If you find more evidence to indicate Mr. Foxx, I'm willing to go that route, but I'm going forward with this operation plan until there's a reason to stop."

"I'll let you know what we find." Oz returned to his desk across the room and huddled with Bronson for a few moments.

Liz refocused on creating her plan. She needed more information on Tillie and used the girl's password from the pink phone to log into her informant's private account, then scrolled through her pictures and video clips.

Multiple images displayed in a grid pattern, with one of Mr. Foxx's business partners as the primary focus. In some, Judd Thoreau posed with a group or was the main attraction of a candid shot as if he didn't know he was being photographed.

The last image taken of Judd was before Tillie was killed and was the same one Liz had seen before. Tillie stood next to him, beaming like a smitten school-girl. Judd had to be the man Greasy Lee mentioned in his interrogation.

A wave of nausea washed over Liz with the discovery. The man was old enough to be Tillie's father, but if they were a couple, then he took advantage of his business partner's young daughter despite being married to another woman. Men like Mr. Thoreau made her want to remain single forever.

She'd have to tell Oz. Maybe he was right. Maybe the case warranted a bit more investigation before she placed her life on the sacrificial table.

Liz pushed back from her desk, crossed the room and pulled up a chair next to him. "Hey, can I show you something?"

Oz hesitated for a moment, then moved to the side, giving her access to his keyboard. With a punch of a few keys, she pulled up Tillie's images. "Recognize this guy?"

"Yeah. That's Judd Thoreau, business partner of Jeremiah's."

"Tillie has over fifty images of him in her private account. Why do you think that is?"

Oz clicked back to a page of financial documents he'd discovered. "Maybe it's the same reason we have receipts and street cam footage of Judd and Tillie entering several restaurants together on multiple occasions."

"So you think he's her married boyfriend too?"

"I think it's a good chance."

"Then I guess we know who we need to interrogate next."

Oz lifted his pen and wrote a couple of notes on the

pad of paper. "Does that mean you're willing to hold off on the sting operation?"

The concern in his eyes softened her resolve. "Let's see what Judd has to say for himself, and then I'll let you know."

"Good." Oz smiled.

She wasn't thrilled at putting her plans on hold, however she'd give his investigative skills a chance. If Judd Thoreau lawyered up, she'd move forward with or without Oz's help.

"Any idea where our suspect is at this hour?"

"I sent out a BOLO about thirty minutes ago. Officers are canvassing his home, work and nearby bars, but so far, nothing. We'll find him."

Liz stifled a yawn. "We should check with Mr. Foxx too. If they're business partners, then he might know where Judd is."

"It's getting late, and we've not had much sleep in the past few days. Let me drop you off at home. We'll both get some rest and start again first thing in the morning."

Liz agreed, and they headed back to her apartment for the first time in what felt like forever. She couldn't wait to take a hot shower and climb into her own bed. Oz wound through her small section of town past the cute dress shops, art galleries and a delicious bakery, then pulled to the curb in front of her building.

"Thanks for the lift." She unbuckled her seat belt.

"I'm sorry about earlier."

She paused.

"I want you to know I'm not questioning your ability as an undercover cop, Liz. I know you're good. I've read the reports and see the number of cases you've closed." He looked out at the street in front of them and tapped his thumbs against the steering wheel. "Truth is—I like you, and I don't want to see you get hurt."

His honest admission took her by surprise, and she placed her hand on his arm. "I'm not going to get hurt. Like you said, I'm good at my job, and no matter how we end up catching this person, even if something bad happens to me, the most important thing is he's in prison, unable to hurt anyone else."

She pulled the handle, stepped from the car and disappeared up the stairs to her second-floor apartment. Oz's words stuck with her as she walked toward the police guard stationed at the door. A renewed lightness filled her exhausted body with his admission. She liked him too, and maybe after all this was over, they could figure out a way to make a relationship work.

"Detective Burke. I'll go in and do a quick sweep inside for you."

She checked the guard's name badge located above his right pocket. "Thank you, Officer Greer, but I can handle my own sweep tonight."

Liz inserted the key into the lock. "Although if I yell for you, then feel free to burst through the door."

She stepped inside her apartment, locked the door behind her and kept the lights off, thankful for the solitude. With a kick of her boots to the floor, she removed her gun and badge, then placed them on the entry table and headed toward her bedroom. She inhaled a deep breath, relishing the sweet smell of her air freshener and another familiar scent—pipe smoke.

Shivers crawled up her spine. It couldn't be.

"Hello, Liz." The deep male voice stopped her in her tracks.

Her muscles tensed as the hum of a powered wheelchair echoed from the shadows. She turned, never expecting to see her ex-boyfriend again.

Light from a neighboring building cast a glow across his face. "It's been a while."

Trey.

EIGHT

Liz tugged at the wrinkled pink flannel shirt she still wore—a stark contrast to Trey's suit, tie and Italian leather shoes. He never dressed nice when they were together. Then again, she'd never looked this bad when they dated either. Her hair was a mess, her makeup was gone and a hole in her sock revealed unmanicured toes.

"What are you doing here?" Liz took a few steps backward, noted her gun was within reach and switched on the lamp next to the door. The guard was only one scream away if she needed him.

Multiple times she'd tried to leave Trey. He always manipulated her thoughts and heart, pulling her right back in to the same vulnerable position. She never intended to be the victim of an abusive man and would've laughed at anyone who told her otherwise. Yet, even after all this time, the shame from her past rushed back with a vengeance upon seeing him—still as handsome as ever despite the blackness of his heart.

Trey inched forward in his chair and swirled some amber liquid around the bottom of one of her low-ball glasses from the dishwasher. Whiskey on the rocks was his all-time favorite drink when they were together, but she never kept any in her home. Maybe he brought the liquor with him.

"I needed to see you." He raised his glass in the air. "Don't worry. It's only tea from your fridge. I hope you don't mind that I drank some. You always did have a knack for the right amount of sweetness."

She ignored his attempt to compliment her. "How'd you find me?"

He lifted the glass and downed the final bit. "I still have a few connections with some of your friends. They told me where you were."

He always had a way of getting people to talk, even those who were supposed to be loyal. "And my apartment? Did someone give you a key?"

Ice cubes clinked when he sat the glass on a side table. She didn't remind him to use a coaster. Past comments like those had often triggered violent outcomes. Funny how nightmarish memories arose with one sound. She thought she'd released all her anger, but familiar rage smoldered just beneath the surface.

"I have my ways."

"Answer the question, Trey."

He avoided a response and rolled a few inches closer. "Why do you have a police guard outside?"

"It's a long story." Liz took another step toward the door and inhaled a deep breath to calm the rapid beat of her heart. She ignored the instant ringing in her ears. Now was not the moment to panic. He showed no fear of her, even after she'd paralyzed him with a shot meant to kill, but every fiber of her being wanted to flee as far away as possible.

"I've got time."

He folded his muscled arms across his chest, his biceps twice as large as when she last saw him. His dedication to the gym had paid off from the looks of his massive upper body, but it accentuated the small proportion of his paralyzed legs.

She kept at least a five-foot distance. One good grasp and she'd be in the physical fight of her life. "Tell me how you got into my place."

"Your neighbor let me in. I told her I was an old friend, and when people see a man in a wheelchair, they take pity. Their looks used to bother me, but once I realized my injury might help me in the business world, I embraced my new lot in life. The wheels soften people's demeanor before negotiations even start, and by the time I'm done with my pitch, they don't even know what hit them. They assume I'm not a threat."

"Are you? A threat?"

He smiled. "Of course not." The length of his hair was longer than before, and his typical five o'clock stubble had evolved into a fully groomed beard. "I can understand why you might think so. Even though you were the one who almost killed me that night. You probably think I'm here for revenge."

"The thought crossed my mind."

"I've changed, Liz. Since the accident, I've had a lot of time to think and get my life straight. My counselor said I needed to make amends and move forward in life. That's why I'm here—to apologize."

His gaze met hers. She'd heard those words before. Multiple times. But nothing ever changed. He still abused her and drank himself into oblivion, while she locked herself in dark closets to escape his wrath. She bit back a chuckle. "Oh, please. Do you really expect me to buy this act?"

"It's not an act. I'm being honest."

"Like all the other times? Surely you can understand why I'm prone not to believe you."

"True. But this time I'm being sincere."

Her fingers fumbled for the dead bolt. One twist and the lock would open. Her officer could enter, when needed, and she was sure she'd need him. "So you met Ms. Tillman?"

"A delightful lady, that one. Cute little dog too. Once I told her how long we'd known each other, she got quite chatty."

Still deceitful, manipulative and using people to gain information against her. He won over their colleagues with his charm. They'd tell him anything he wanted to know, and he used their words as a reason to hit her.

"And you thought that was okay? Why would you think talking to my neighbors and entering my home when I'm not here would be acceptable?"

He held up his hands. "You're right. I'm sorry. I should've called first. I just figured you would never agree to see me if I called."

"Good guess."

"So instead of asking for permission, I decided on the ask-forgiveness route. That's why I'm here, even though I can see that absolution is not something you're ready to give. I'd hoped by saying these things in person, you might be more inclined to accept my apology."

He wheeled a bit closer. She unlocked the door. No way was she going to let him get too close or block her only exit. He stopped.

His gaze shifted to the lock. "I didn't come here to hurt you, Liz. I know what I did in the past was evil. I get why you're scared, but what I did to you, to us, is not who I am now. Back then I was consumed by alcohol and pills, my jealousy drove me to do horrible things. I couldn't stand the thought of someone taking you from me or if another man looked at or talked to you. That was wrong. I was wrong. I'm not asking for your forgiveness, but I wanted to tell you how sorry I am. That's why I came."

"No ulterior motive?"

"None."

The tension in her shoulders and neck relaxed a little. He seemed sincere, and she was an expert at reading his moods. Her only means of self-preservation.

"Our time together wasn't all bad, was it?" He shot her a shy smile.

A flash of the Trey she fell in love with returned, but she'd never let him back into her life, not after the pain she went through to escape his wrath. Their time together was done. "Maybe you should go. You've said your piece."

"You won't even acknowledge any of the good between us?"

"Does it matter? What we had is over. No sense in reminiscing."

"It matters to me. I'd like to know that there is at least one good memory for you."

Liz released the doorknob and wiped her sweaty palm against her jeans. "I suppose we had some fun in the beginning, but after your promotion to the homicide unit, things took a turn for the worst, and I was the brunt of all the bad in you. Every night we were together, I lived in fear of being hit or assaulted. When you didn't come home because of your philandering ways, I didn't even care because it meant one night of peace. One night of not having to hide in a dark locked closet so I'd be safe."

Tears streamed down her cheeks, and she swiped at them, angry she let them fall. He loved preying on her weaknesses and using her shame against her, but these tears weren't for him. Instead, they cleansed her soul.

He wheeled forward, and she reached over, placing her hand on her gun. "Don't come any closer. I'm not that girl anymore, and if you ever lay a hand on me again, I promise…I won't miss."

"I'm so sorry. There aren't enough words to excuse my addiction. The cases we worked in Homicide were disturbing on so many levels. I drank to forget the images in my head, but that's no excuse for hurting you."

Liz remained close to her weapon. "You almost killed me."

"And you me."

She couldn't argue there. He was in a wheelchair because of her. "I never would've pulled the trigger if I'd had any other choice. I tried to get you to stop. Why didn't you just stop?"

His eyes glistened with tears. He wheeled his chair to the side so she couldn't see. "If I could go back and change things, I would, but that's not an option. Since I got sober and started therapy, things are slowly improving. I feel like I'm getting my life back—well, not exactly the same one I had before but some sense of purpose to life."

If only she could say the same, but settling into Mills Creek had been harder than expected. She didn't have any friends, and her new detective job hadn't been easy. Liz had wanted a fresh start and got one until Tillie was killed. The violence brought back too many memories she'd fought to put behind her. She changed the subject.

"What are you doing now?"

"After the accident, I started a private security firm. We're doing pretty well. We have some government projects, which benefited our growth, and we're expanding."

"Not here though, right?"

An awkward pause filled the space between them. Trey wheeled to her window. "Your neighbor told me about your friend getting killed. Said she read it in the paper and had met Tillie once before. How are you holding up?"

The avoidance of her question spoke volumes. "Your company's not coming to Mills Creek, is it, Trey?"

"I can't discuss any of my company's future contracts, but hypothetically, what would you say if I was?"

"I'd move again. We can't be in the same town. If you're sincere about your apology and wanting to make amends, then give me Mills Creek, without you."

He smiled and motioned toward the door. "I'd best be going, but if anyone can find who killed your friend, you can. You're an amazing detective."

Compliments always preceded the past storms Trey stirred up in her life, and he never flattered anyone unless he wanted something in return. More was coming, and she feared the revelation would be worse than his past punches.

"Take care of yourself, Liz, and stay out of trouble. I remember how you like to take risks, but sometimes life is best navigated with a bit of caution instead of emotion."

His friendly banter and unsolicited advice unnerved

her on so many levels, but she opened the door to let him out. The police guard startled at Trey's presence and reached for his gun, but Liz stopped him. He stepped to the side after she explained.

"Thanks for talking with me." Trey turned his wheelchair to face her again after rolling into the hallway. "I know I was probably the last person you expected to see tonight, but since I was going to be in town this weekend, I figured now was as good a time as any. I am surprised you didn't throw me out."

"The thought crossed my mind."

He moved farther down the hallway, then stopped again. "About your friend…if there's one thing I learned while working Homicide, it's that most murderers only kill for one of three reasons—love, money or power. Follow those trails and you'll figure out who's behind Tillie's death."

"How'd you know her name?"

He shrugged his shoulders. "Who doesn't know Jeremiah Foxx's daughter? She's made national headlines before and not in a good way."

"What do you mean?"

"Do an internet search. Her missing person's case from a few years ago is bound to pop up. Very interesting read."

"And your little visit has nothing to do with her murder?"

"Other than coming to see you, I'm attending Mayor DeMoss's reelection campaign fundraiser this weekend. Seems it's the ticket to have. Even the Foxx's are going to be there to fill her coffers with large campaign donations."

"But you don't live here."

"Don't worry, Liz. I can always hire another person to manage our satellite office. You won't even know I'm around." He pressed his chair handle forward and tossed her a wave. "Have a good night."

Liz waited for Trey to load into the elevator before heading back into her apartment, where she closed the door and locked the dead bolt. He knew where she lived and planned to expand his company into her new town. Same old Trey. He may be sober, but he always found a way to wreak havoc in her life even if he visited under the guise of an apology.

A loud engine revved outside her window, and she looked down to the alley below. Other than a stray cat perched on top of a trash can licking the remnants of his dinner from his paws, the side road was empty.

Liz's fingers brushed across the disengaged latch on top of the lower pane window. When had she unlocked it? The last time she'd been in her apartment was before Tillie died—the night of her cousin's Christmas party. She was sure they were latched then.

She moved through each room checking all her windows and doors. Only the one leading to her fire escape was breeched, but by who? Trey couldn't climb the stairs to her second-floor apartment, but he had the funds to hire someone else to do his dirty work.

Maybe Oz was right. This could be her past coming back to haunt her. Tomorrow she'd visit Ms. Tillman and ask for her extra key back.

Oz never expected Trey to exit Liz's apartment complex when he did a quick drive-by to check on her, but what other man would roll his wheelchair into a black van after leaving her building. He identified Trey's photo with one from the company's main webpage for an official ID.

Now Oz stood beside the third floor windows of the abandoned warehouse across from McManus Security's back alley and twisted the night vision scope into focus. Painted on the side of a luxury black van was the company's logo. Trey McManus was in Mills Creek and if he almost killed her once, then he'd be willing to commit the crime again.

The police guard posted at Liz's door reported their visit lasted about fifteen minutes from the time she arrived home until she escorted him out. Liz should've tossed the man out on his keister as soon as she realized he was in her place.

"Thanks for meeting me," Oz said when Bronson walked into the abandoned warehouse space, three floors up with a direct line of sight of Trey's new security building. "Looks like Liz's ex has decided to open up a satellite office here in Mills Creek."

"That's not a coincidence."

"Nope. Anyone see you come inside?"

"I took the back stairs like you said." His friend joined him at the window and pulled out a camera with a telephoto lens attached. "So, we're surveilling Liz's ex? Are you sure this isn't personal?"

"He tracked her down and my guess is he's up to no good. She moved here to get away from him. One too many beatings."

His partner clicked an image of the license plate tag, which automatically uploaded into a shared file. Oz enlarged the photo for a better view. "Looks like he's waiting on someone."

"And we're going to find out who." Oz moved to an

adjacent window for a better view. "Liz's guard said Trey was inside her apartment when she got home."

"Did he not do a security check before she went inside?"

"He tried but she pulled rank on him and insisted she could manage a simple security sweep. When all remained quiet, he figured everything was fine." Oz focused his night scope lens. "Thankfully the visit was cordial."

"I suppose that's a good thing."

"This time. If he's on the up and up, then why didn't he meet her in a public place or give her a call? This has power play written all over it. Especially now that he's meeting someone in a dark alley at midnight."

"We might find out sooner than we thought." Bronson aimed the camera in the opposite direction and snapped a few pics.

A black SUV with darkened windows pulled in behind Trey's van. The driver who exited the vehicle wore a baseball cap and kept his back to the camera. Oz crossed to the door. "Stay here. Try to get a shot of the guy's face."

"Where are you going?"

"I want a closer look."

"Not a good idea. If they see you—"

"They won't."

Oz took the stairs two at a time until he reached the bottom floor. Trash and discarded beer cans littered the exit. Rats squeaked in the shadows from the darkened corridor. He crept to the end of the hallway, out a back door close to where the vehicles were parked and ducked down behind a dumpster. He fought the urge to gag from scents of rotting food mixed with the foul odor of a dead animal carcass.

From the edge of the container, Oz focused his scope to the perfect line of sight. Shadows moved inside the van, but the visitor didn't emerge. "Come on. Step out."

Something scuttled behind Oz. Probably another rat looking for a meal. He refocused and raised the scope to his eye. A man stepped from the van backward, still chatting with Trey on the inside. "Turn around," Oz whispered.

A noise clicked behind him, and a strong grip landed on his shoulder. Oz turned, ready to fight but liquid sprayed into his eyes and face. Instant pain burned down his throat. Pepper spray, no doubt. He raised his arm to block the chemical onslaught. Male voices spoke around him, but he couldn't identify the blurred faces. He squeezed his eyes shut, trying to block out the intense pain.

A hard punch struck his side, knocking the breath from his lungs. He curled and tried to inhale. More burning ensued while several kicks landed against his torso.

He fought back blind as best he could until an object hit the side of his head. Oz crumpled to the asphalt, giving up any attempt to defend himself.

A loud siren woke Oz from his unconscious state. Two men he did not know hovered over him flashing a light into his eyes still on fire from the assault.

"Detective Kelly? You're in an ambulance on the way to the hospital. My name is Ben and this is my teammate, Matt. We're paramedics and are going to take care of you."

Matt drew up liquid into a syringe, then injected the medicine into an IV attached to Oz's arm.

"My partner, Bronson?"

"He's following in the car behind us. Thanks to him we were able to get to you in time. We're headed to Mills Creek Memorial. You took a pretty good beating, and we want to make sure you don't have any internal bleeding."

The ambulance jostled his body over sewer grates and railroad tracks. Oz closed his eyes again. Every muscle ached and his head throbbed. He wasn't sure if most of the pain was from the beating he'd endured or the hard backboard underneath him. Both were excruciating, but the meds took effect and helped.

At the hospital, doctors cleared his cervical spine of any injuries and moved him into a secure room with a softer mattress. A knock tapped against the door, and Liz entered with Bronson on her heels.

She slipped her fingers into Oz's hand, the best touch he had felt in a long time. "I heard what happened. Weren't you supposed to head home and get some sleep, not take down Clive and his gang?"

"Clive?"

Bronson moved to the end of his bed. "They met with Trey."

He squeezed her fingers. "Why was McManus at your apartment? What did he want, Liz?"

"To apologize."

"Doubtful. That was his cover, and after the beating I received, I want him brought in and questioned." He turned to Bronson. "Put out a BOLO on him."

"You know I'm not one to defend the man." She took a seat in a chair by his bedside and released his hand.

"But the images Bronson took show Trey rolling out of the van and stopping the assault. He wasn't behind this."

Bronson stepped forward and pulled his camera from the backpack. "Here's what I caught. Thankfully, I'd switched to video. We have your attackers on tape."

After flipping through a couple of clips, Oz handed the camera back. "My vision's still too blurry to make out any details."

"Three men ambushed you from the other car," Liz said.

Bronson clicked through the images. "They were with the East Mountain Mafia. They saw you come out of the building and thought you were a threat to Clive. By the time I reached you, they were gone."

Oz sat up in bed. "Then if Trey McManus is working with the East Mountain Mafia, he's involved. Where'd he get money to hire them?"

"When he was in my apartment, he told me he owns a private security firm, and they're doing well financially."

"So the man has money and holds a grudge against you. That only leaves one question. Did he kill Tillie?"

Liz sat back in her chair. "Oz, I know when Trey is lying, and tonight his apology seemed sincere. Although I'll keep him in my sights. I don't trust him either, but he has no reason to kill Tillie."

"Except to get back at you."

"If he wanted to hurt me, he'd hurt *me*, not her."

"The timing of his conversion is a bit suspicious, don't ya think?" Her defensiveness annoyed Oz. Trey abused her. Funny how her memory seemed to fade after his visit. With money and ties to gangs of assassins, Trey had motive and means to attack Liz or anyone else who got in his way, like Tillie.

Another knock tapped on the door and Sergeant Wright walked into the room. "Man, you look awful. Do you need some time off or—"

Oz waved a hand. "I'm fine. Nothing a shower, some food and a good night's sleep won't fix."

"Glad to hear it because I need you both for our next operation."

"For this case?" Liz asked.

Two nurses passed by the room, laughing at a private joke. Sergeant Wright closed the door. "We have intel on Judd Thoreau, and I need you to bring him in. After officers conducted a search of his place, we found a match to what we believe is the murder weapon that killed Tillie. The gun is in the lab for testing, but it's the same brand and caliber. What I need from you two is to attend the BBQ fundraiser for Mayor DeMoss on Saturday. Intel said that Mr. Thoreau plans to be there."

"That's a pretty public place to show up if you know the cops are looking for you," Oz said.

"We think he's meeting with someone, and sometimes it's easier to get lost in a crowd."

Liz pulled out her phone and typed on the screen. "I'll go. Why not let Oz rest for a few days? I'll bring in Judd."

"Not alone." Oz wasn't about to let her get him sidelined. "Trey might be there and even though he helped tonight, I'm not convinced of his innocence."

"We have officers looking for the men who attacked you tonight and McManus came by to give his statement on your behalf. He's not our main focus. Our objective for this weekend is to locate Judd and arrest him for Tillie's murder."

Oz reached for a cup of water and took a sip. "Count me in."

"Good. The fundraiser is scheduled for Saturday in the Mills Creek town square. That gives you one day to rest up."

Liz stopped typing. "The mayor's election is in two months. Trey mentioned Jeremiah Foxx would be there."

Sergeant Wright looked at his phone and scrolled down. "He's on the list. I want the two of you to talk to as many people as you can. Get hard evidence Judd was having an affair with Foxx's daughter, which will give us an airtight case against him with the murder weapon in play now. Dismiss any hearsay and gossip."

Oz hit the call button. He was tired of being in the hospital and wanted his discharge papers. He hoped the operation would give him something to think about besides Liz.

"By the way—" Sergeant Wright turned back to Oz before walking out the door "—I'm putting you both in one of our safe houses until this is over. You can work there, but with the EMM coming after you both, we need to be careful." He faced Bronson. "Can I see you out in the hall for a moment?"

His partner exited the room, leaving Oz and Liz alone. She avoided his gaze and continued to scroll on her phone. Maybe she didn't want to stay with him again. After their romantic encounter at the lake house, he wasn't sure he trusted himself either.

"I can stay somewhere else if you want," she said without looking at him.

"Of course not. We need to work on the case, and that

would be hard to do if we were in separate locations." He pushed up from the bed but the room spun and he swayed forward. Liz moved to his side and helped him back to a reclined position. "Careful. You've had a head injury and if you sit up too fast, then you might pass out."

He held up a hand. "I just need a minute to let my equilibrium balance out. That's all." Every muscle in his body ached, but the throbbing in his head was the worst.

"I guess it's a good thing I'll be staying with you. Looks like you'll need me there."

He was used to ignoring pain when solving a case. "Give me a day or two and I'll be fine. I don't need a nurse."

Her teasing smile faded. She tucked her phone in her pocket and folded her arms across her chest. "Got it. We're only there to work."

"Exactly. Tillie's killer is still out there, and if we want to find them, then we must keep everything professional."

"I can do that."

"Do you mind stepping out into the hallway?"

She looked at him, a bit of defiance tilting up her chin. "I don't think you should be alone. You might get dizzy again."

He motioned for the green patient bag hanging on the hook beside her. "Problem is, I need to get dressed, and I really don't want you to see me in a backless hospital gown."

"Oh. Right." Liz handed him his clothes. "I'll be right outside."

Once he was alone, Oz removed his jeans from the bag and slipped them on. "It's only a few days. After we arrest Judd, you can go back to your place and Liz will go back to hers. You can handle anything for a few days."

He'd lived the fairy tale with his wife and look how that ended. He couldn't go through that kind of pain and grief again, but the kiss with Liz challenged his determination to remain single. If only the hit to his head had made him forget that moment, then maybe sharing the same space with her wouldn't be so hard.

NINE

Bluegrass music blared across six town blocks in Mills Creek, unhindered by the barriers sectioning off the area's largest car show and festival of the holiday season. Vintage vehicles decked out in reindeer antlers and grill wreaths lined the streets. The town had transformed into a throwback of Christmas past and people milled about, waving at friends, drinking hot cocoa while standing in line at the mayor's photo booth. Purchase one selfie for fifty dollars and constituents received a cheap Santa hat along with the politician's favor.

Liz walked past the mayor's tent, and the woman called her name. "Can we talk for a moment?"

They'd never spoken before, and Liz couldn't imagine what they'd have to discuss, but she obliged the woman's request. Mayor DeMoss wore a jewel-toned red top, black slacks and heeled boots. Couldn't be more than thirty-five with dark hair and eyes. "Nice to meet you, Mayor DeMoss."

"Likewise." The woman had a firm handshake. "How are you liking the festival?"

"I just arrived so I'm still taking it all in, but it seems

like everyone's having a good time. Not a bad turnout for your campaign."

"This does ease my mind a bit with the upcoming runoff election in two months. Of course, just because the people show up for a good time, doesn't mean they'll make it to the polls."

"True."

The mayor stepped off to the side away from listening ears and motioned for Liz to follow. "I'm putting together a private security team, and I'm looking for a strong female as team lead. You've made quite the reputation for yourself at the department since arriving, and I think you'd be a good fit."

"You want me to head up your security team?" Liz shook her head. "I wouldn't think in a midsize town you'd need that level of protection."

"Do you see that man over there at the front of the booth?"

Liz followed her gaze. Tall, gray-headed in plain clothes with the bulge of a weapon on his side. "I do."

"He's retiring and said he'd see me through the election, but the time has come to move to Florida with his wife. They've dreamed of living in the warmer weather for a long time. I need a new lead and about three others underneath you."

"I'm flattered, but I'm not sure private security is my forte. I work better in a department."

"I'll triple your salary."

Liz hesitated for a moment with her statement. A shadowed look flashed across the woman's face, fear in her eyes. "Is there something you're not saying? Are you in danger?"

The mayor's gaze darted around to a few people, then

back to her. "A politician always has enemies. Either someone who disagrees with her policies or another who wants her spot."

"But you're a mayor of a smaller town, not the president of the United States."

"Doesn't matter. There's always someone waiting in the wings. Will you help me?"

"I'm happy where I am, but thank you for thinking of me."

"Of course. If you change—"

"Mayor DeMoss, I'm so sorry to interrupt, but the line is getting backed up." A handsome man in his twenties stood with his small laptop in hand. "I don't want people to get restless."

"Of course. I'll be right there." She faced Liz again when he moved away. "I wish you'd change your mind, but if not, then perhaps I'll go with that handsome partner of yours. What's his name again?"

"Oz?"

"Yes, like the wizard." Her gaze turned dreamy. "I must get back to work. Enjoy the festival."

Mayor DeMoss returned to the masses with a red-lipped smile plastered on her face. Liz would give the offer some more thought after the festival, but right now she needed to find Oz.

Liz skirted the edge of an elevated platform located in the town center and almost caught a square dancer's foot to the top of her head. The girl flashed a smile, jostled her red-and-green-plaid skirt to the lively jingle bell beat, then slung her other foot around in a whirligig pattern before sashaying off to another dancer.

A loud whoop echoed from the right side underneath

a Christmas cornhole tournament banner. Oz high-fived Bronson, who seemed to have made the final score.

The referee moved their team name up a space on the scoreboard. The "Corn Chips" were now in second place. A few other players lined up next to them, all looking a bit defeated as she approached. Before making her presence known, Liz watched Oz shake hands with all the other players. His amazing smile filled his entire countenance with an easy joy that drew people to him.

"You used to look at me that way," Trey said from behind her.

Liz turned and spotted her ex seated in his wheelchair, his lips tinted blue from the roll of cotton candy he was eating. "You used to be happy like him."

"I guess people change sometimes."

She hoped Oz never changed, but how could she be sure he wouldn't? Trey was right. They'd been happy once before he gave in to his darkness. Liz pointed at the blue treat he held. "If you buy the pink one, then your mouth won't look like a Smurf."

"I like the blue. Reminds me of when I was a kid at the fair. Want some?"

She snatched a piece from the edge he hadn't touched and popped the treat into her mouth. "I was hoping after our discussion the other night you'd forgo the mayor's fundraiser and head back to Charlotte."

"And miss all this?" He held out his arms as if embracing the festival, then took another bite of his candy. "I like the place. It's quaint and quiet. Everyone's friendly. I think I could find some peace here."

His words unnerved her, but she wasn't surprised. He always manipulated and tried to control every situation, especially if she was involved. He hadn't changed. "I'm sure there are other towns where you could find peace."

"But not near as much money. Mayor DeMoss awarded my business a government contract to bring our services here to the local college. She wants to start a security training program."

"Really? That's interesting." The woman was up to something, and Liz wasn't sure she liked the sound of the project. "Seems a bit of an overkill for our town. It's not like we're Charlotte or Atlanta where the mayor would need a large police force."

"From my understanding, if she wins this election, then she has some policies she wants to implement that could bring out the wolves. That's why she wants to hire us."

"Are you the reason she made me a job offer to lead her security team?"

"She asked who I thought would do a good job. You came to mind."

Liz crossed her arms. "I should've known."

The position made sense now. Of course, Trey had manipulated the mayor. He always had a way of making people do what he wanted. I guess she had her decision and didn't need the rest of the week to turn down the job.

"You need to take the position, Liz. These kinds of opportunities don't come along often, and I promise to stay out of your way. I'll even return to Charlotte if you promise to take the job."

He didn't get to do this anymore. Trey was no longer a part of her life, and there was no way she was taking a position that would make her indebted to him. "I'm not interested. Do what you want with your life, Trey, but kindly stay out of mine."

Liz turned and walked over to Oz, trying to push the news from her head. At least the day's festivities provided a distraction. "Well, I've seen it all now. Detective Kelly—Corn Chip extraordinaire."

He gave a small bow. "What can I say? The game is fun to play."

"Love the name."

"Yeah. We had to come up with something quick and I was eating a bag of Fritos at the time."

"Do you ride a motorcycle too on your way to the Cornhole Championships or get a tattoo to commemorate your victories?" She flashed a teasing smile up at him.

"Detective Burke. Do I sense a hint of mockery in your tone? Just so you know, I win money playing in these tournaments."

"And that's why no one can ever reach you on the weekends."

Oz leaned forward and picked up the bags Bronson tossed at his feet. "I've always answered your calls."

"And I'm grateful, but while you were playing your game, did you happen to notice the growing number of East Mountain Mafia members to your right?"

Oz raised his square beanbag in front of his face, then swung his arm with a perfect throw hitting his target for the score. "I saw them. As well as your ex. I thought he went back home."

"Me too. We thought wrong."

"Not sure why he or the EMM would be at a political fundraiser."

"Maybe to keep the mayor in their pocket. A little

palm-greasing can go a long way when one of them gets arrested. As for Trey, his company received a government contract from our beloved mayor to teach his security program at the local college."

"So he's moving here?"

"Not only that but he told DeMoss to hire me to lead her new private security team."

Oz tossed the bag and missed. "Are you going to?"

"And let him control my life again? Never."

A gentle breeze shifted, and the scent of smoked brisket filled the air. Liz's tummy growled. "I think I'm gonna go grab a barbecue. You want anything while I'm over in the food court?"

"We've got a break coming up, but I want to practice a bit more with Bronson and then I'll meet ya in fifteen. Is that okay?"

She nodded and followed the mouthwatering smell, then placed her order. Pounds of meat sizzled on a large black smoker positioned behind the tent. Maybe some food would help calm her nerves.

The combination of her growing attraction to Oz and the reappearance of Trey increased her anxiety. She didn't trust her ex, his manipulative offer or his prolonged stay in Mills Creek. The entire situation reeked of trouble.

Liz picked up her order, complete with hand-cut french fries, and wound into the empty alleyway where customers sat at shaded picnic tables to eat their food. A live band played nearby, almost drowning out the children's squeals of glee as they slid down large inflatables slides and jumped into an enormous ball pit.

Mayor DeMoss spared no expense for her fundraiser or pet projects, which often took precedent over the true needs of her constituents, but the townspeople seemed to have put their political differences aside today.

Liz spotted one open seat next to Miranda Foxx, Tillie's mother. She sat at a table by herself. Her daughter's murder remained prominent in the news, and although most people supported the woman, they also avoided drama. The town wanted no part of any scandal, but Liz never shied away from a loner, especially when she had a job to do. Miranda's insight into her daughter's affair might prove valuable. Those kinds of secrets never stayed hidden, and Liz seized the opening.

"Pretty amazing fundraiser, don't ya think?" She sat her food on the picnic table and took her seat.

The woman flicked a cold stare in her direction. "Mayor DeMoss always throws extravagant parties. And the town loves her for it."

"But you don't?"

"Excuse me?"

Liz took a sip of her drink. "From your tone, my guess is there's no love lost between you two."

Miranda hesitated as if trying to decide whether to answer. "Mayor DeMoss is fine."

Liz popped a fry into her mouth and let the hard, angry silence settle between them for a moment. "Well, at least it's a nice day. How have you been? I'm sure losing Tillie hasn't been easy."

Tears welled in the woman's eyes. "I lost my daughter a long time ago, Detective. My daily life without her hasn't changed."

"Still. The hope of reconciliation is gone too."

"Hard to lose something I never had. Tillie made it very clear the last time she saw me that there was no hope of reconciliation. Not after what happened."

Liz took a sip of her drink. "Do you mean with Judd?"

The woman's face paled when she mentioned the man's name. "How do you know about that?"

"I'm a detective. It's my job. And—" she chewed the bite of her sandwich a bit slower, giving time for Miranda's thoughts to run wild "—I don't think their affair was much of a secret."

"That's not—"

Someone strong bumped into Liz, pushing her body forward. She shoved back, but the man's grip was firm. An EMM tattoo peeked out from underneath his folded-up shirtsleeve. Clive Hawkins stood over her and pulled on her arm, his grip tighter than she liked. "I need to talk to you in private."

She jerked her arm loose. "I'm surrounded by the entire Mills Creek police force. Do you really want to make a scene?"

Clive looked back over his shoulder toward a grouping of buildings. She followed his gaze. Someone moved on top of the roof. "Get down."

His strong hand shoved her underneath the table as shots fired.

Bullets dusted up around them, and the man covered her body with his. She struggled against him.

"Hold still."

"Let me go."

He pulled a smoke grenade from his pocket and activated the trigger. A white cloud enveloped them, providing a screen.

"I need to get you to cover. Once the smoke clears, the sniper on top of the building across the street will have a straight shot, and we gotta be outta here by then."

More gunfire popped around them.

"I need to stop him." She wiped a drop of moisture from her cheek. She looked at her fingers, now stained with blood from the wooden slats above her. Miranda's body was slumped over the tabletop, unmoving. Liz reached up and grabbed the woman's limp arm and pulled down. Her torso fell like a sack of potatoes onto the bench seat, a fatal gunshot wound to her head.

Clive loosened his grip when the barrage of bullets paused. "Time to move."

He pulled her out from under the picnic table, and they ran for the closest building at the corner of Main and Sycamore Street. More gunfire chased them, but they made a clean escape.

Liz scanned the chaos for Oz. She spotted him at the end of another street, one building over. If she could get to him, then they could work together to stop the sniper.

She turned around to thank Clive, but he was nowhere to be found. Why of all people would *he* protect her? Maybe he wasn't lying about being hired to keep her alive, after all.

A side door behind her exited into the alley. She pulled on the handle, but it was locked. If she could get through the interior of the building, she could rejoin Oz. Several more businesses lined the street, but only one had a public restroom sign displayed above. She entered, ran down the tiled hallway with her weapon drawn and stepped out the other side. More gunfire erupted. Liz flattened against the brick.

"Oz."

He looked behind him and gestured for her to stay put. When the gunfire subsided again, he moved to her side. His eyes widened when he saw blood on her clothes. "Are you hurt?"

"It's not mine. Miranda Foxx was shot while I was near her."

"Fatal?"

She nodded.

"But you're not hit?"

"Clive shoved me underneath the picnic table right before the shooting started."

The lines in his face tensed. "He protected you?"

"Seems that way."

"Guess he wasn't lying about keeping you alive."

"Guess not."

Oz motioned toward the street. "Our team is positioned around the square, but none of them hold a good position. We're the closest. The shooter is located on the building roof across the street. I think we can make the distance during the reloads. There's a fire escape up the side of the building to the roof."

Liz gripped her weapon a bit tighter and wished she had worn her bulletproof vest. Questioning people for information was supposed to be an uncomplicated operation not requiring Kevlar. "Then let's go."

"Stay close to me."

She ran across the street. A burst of ammo bounced around them, the ping of each shot igniting a boost of adrenaline. When they reached the other side, she flattened her body against the brick wall a little too hard.

Oz breathed heavy beside her. "Let's move to the corner and then up the stairs."

"The shooter knows we're coming, and he's got the advantage. We could split up. I'll go external and you internal?"

Oz tried the door handle. "It's locked."

"Can't we shoot the glass?"

"Unfortunately the sniper picked town hall as his base, and about a year ago the city council voted to upgrade all the windows and doors with bulletproof glass in this building."

"Then the fire escape it is."

Oz's face paled at her words. "We have no other choice."

A low wall circled the roof's perimeter of the four-story building and provided protection for the shooter. His line of sight to the town center threatened anyone still running through the streets to safety. No one had ever expected such a horrific atrocity to occur in Mills Creek.

"Ready?" Maybe if she pushed forward, the adrenaline would overcome his fear of heights. Oz remained underneath the overhang, rounded the corner and stopped at the fire escape. He motioned for Liz to ascend the first level of stairs, still hidden from the sniper's view. Extra caution was warranted when they turned to the outer levels.

"I'll cover you. Go." Oz stepped into view and aimed his weapon at the roof. Liz took the steps two at a time. They followed this pattern until they reached the final vertical ladder to the roof.

Liz flattened against the side of the building. "He'll be waiting for us. Any ideas on how to keep him from shooting my head when I pop up at the top?"

"We wait for backup."

"More people will die before they can get here."

Oz tapped his radio key. "Send in the drone."

A familiar buzz rose into the air and flew vertical toward their location on the fire escape. Liz climbed the ladder, held her position and waited for the drone to provide an opportunity.

Clicks of reloading and heavy footsteps thumped toward the edge of the roofline. The sniper must've heard the drone and fired a shot. The robotic bird went down, and she peeked up over the edge. He swung his gun in her direction and pulled the trigger again.

Metal debris rained down on Oz as he followed Liz up the ladder and propelled himself onto the concrete roof. Liz chased the suspect and fired three rounds while he approached from the opposite side. He took cover at the corner of the clock tower, then pivoted into position, his weapon raised.

Liz lowered her gun when she saw him. "Looks like he crossed to the other building and pulled the ladder so we couldn't follow. If we hurry, we can catch him below."

"We've already got ground units in place." Oz pressed his radio key. "Suspect, male, dark hair. Approximately six feet, two hundred and ten pounds. Last seen on the roof of Mary's Diner. Believed to be headed to Second Street."

"All available units responding," Dispatch said.

He clipped his radio back to his side, walked to the edge of the adjacent building and took a quick peek into the alleyway below. Officers swarmed the building and breeched the entrances. Oz turned to her. "If he's down there, they'll find him. Looks like every officer in the department is on hand."

"Most active shooters take their own lives before cops can shoot them, but this guy wanted to live. The clock tower served as cover, and he had an extension ladder in place for his planned exit. He's definitely a professional."

"Not surprised there. Our guys will get him."

"I don't know. He was smart. He picked the only building with bulletproof glass, had a fail-proof escape route and took out Tillie's mom. Are there any other victims?"

"Most likely. What are you thinking?"

"That this was a targeted hit, staged to look like a random mass shooting. Most mass murderers want to take as many lives as possible, and he had a prime position for multiple kills, but the only person he hits is Miranda Foxx?"

Oz scanned the streets below. Thousands of people had strolled the town square earlier yet there were no other bodies on the ground. "You're right. I don't see any sign of other fatalities."

"We need to get down there to know for sure. By the way, did you see Jeremiah Foxx at the festival?"

"Now that you mention it, I didn't." He empathized with the familiar pain the man would experience once he learned the news. When Oz's wife died, he never thought he'd recover, and a piece of his soul never did. "Jeremiah Foxx has lost his daughter *and* his wife now."

"Yeah. I'm still surprised he didn't attend. For a businessman who supports Mayor DeMoss, I figured he'd be here."

"That *is* odd. Maybe something came up."

"Or maybe he is behind his wife's death."

Oz took his time descending the fire escape after Liz made her way down. A few more police chases like this and he'd overcome his fear of heights. They made their way into the streets on full alert until they reached the patrolled perimeter. Oz walked toward Bronson, huddled in a group of his colleagues.

"Any news?" Oz asked.

"We got our shooter holed up right now inside of Mary's Diner. Thankfully she'd closed early for the festival so no customers are inside."

"Is SWAT ready to breech? I want this guy and the person who hired him."

"We can't. He's taken a hostage."

Every muscle tensed inside of Oz's body. "Who?"

"Judd Thoreau."

"How'd that happen? We looked for the man all morning and never saw him."

"Not sure, but we have video confirmation they're both inside."

Bronson played the clip for Oz. Judd was duct-taped to a restaurant chair while the shooter paced from the window to the door and back to Judd again, his identity concealed with a ski mask. Bronson stopped the video. "That's all we've got. He spotted the camera and shot it out."

They'd been searching for Judd for over a week. Oz needed the man alive to get to the truth behind Tillie's murder, but scenarios like this usually ended in disaster or worse—with both men dead.

A crisis negotiator arrived by helicopter within thirty minutes from Charlotte, North Carolina. Oz received a text to join Sergeant Wright in the control tent set up outside the building. His superior waved him and Liz over when he entered.

"Kelly and Burke, this is Detective Darla Musgrove. She'll oversee the negotiations to get our hostage released unharmed."

"Nice to meet you." Oz extended his hand.

Musgrove took his, then Liz's. "Likewise."

"I've heard you've made some progress but still no resolution." Oz breathed in the fresh coffee smell from the cup Liz brought with her and wished he'd grabbed some too.

"I wouldn't say that." Darla jotted down a few notes. "We've established contact, and we're waiting to learn the shooter's demands."

He glanced at the monitor. "We can't wait long. Our hostage, Judd Thoreau, is a prominent businessman in the area and one of our primary suspects. I need him alive."

"And the shooter holding him hostage? Any ID on him?" Liz asked.

"Not yet, but we're working on it." The woman enlarged one of the video frames on the screen. "We can't see his face but does anything else look familiar about him?"

Oz stepped in for a closer look but nothing stood out about the man's appearance.

One of her team members approached. "Robot's in place. We should have a live feed now."

Darla pulled out a chair and took her seat at a workstation equipped with multiple computer screens and a landline phone. She turned to two other members standing near her and gave them instructions.

Oz stepped up beside her. "If the abductor sees your robot, then won't he kill our hostage?"

"I've done this hundreds of times, Detective Kelly, and I haven't lost one hostage yet. I don't intend on making today any different."

"I still think we should send SWAT in."

The woman swiveled her chair in his direction. "You want to send them in blind?"

He didn't answer.

"The robot provides us with an audio and video advantage. Most criminals want the robot to leave, which gives us negotiating power."

"What keeps him from just shooting the robot?" Liz asked.

"The Dogo is a small, tactical, robot with weapon capabilities. Most abductors are oblivious to its presence until we have the device in position."

She pointed at her colleague, who held what looked like a rugged digital tablet in his hand. "He operates the robot through the remote control unit. A standard 9mm Glock pistol lives inside the casing and can shoot any target with accuracy. Cameras give us three-hundred-and-sixty-degree views of the structures, and we have audio, allowing us to negotiate with our target."

Darla bounced her gaze back to Oz. "Still want us to send in SWAT first?"

He shook his head and stepped back so she could do her job. Darla gave the command for the robot to enter. With skilled maneuvering, they had a video feed in less than a minute. "Looks like your buddy Judd is all by himself."

"No shooter?" Oz asked.

"He's gone. Judd is duct-taped to a chair in the middle of the room and—" she scrolled through additional street footage on a different monitor "—right here, about twenty minutes ago, our sniper slipped out the back door wearing the very clothes off of Judd's back. Blended in with the crowd until he hopped into a navy sedan with tinted windows and left."

"Another blue sedan?" Liz asked. "Like the one at Tillie's murder?"

"You can send in your SWAT team now, Sergeant Wright."

Oz exited the tent and waited for the bomb dogs and SWAT officers to clear the property for safe entry. He wanted to be the first one to talk to Judd Thoreau. The man came out in handcuffs, wrapped in a blanket, and looked like he'd seen better days. Officers placed him in the back seat of a cruiser.

Before they closed the door, Oz grabbed the edge. He didn't want anything to go wrong with this arrest. With Judd Thoreau's money, connections and lawyers, they had to follow every detail in the book. "Mr. Thoreau, it's nice to finally have you in custody."

"It's not what you think. I didn't kill Tillie."

"We found the murder weapon in your house, looks like you wear a size ten shoe, and you ran. That's not something an innocent man does."

His suspect cast his gaze downward and picked at his fingernails. "I didn't hurt her."

Oz laughed. "Well, you better tell us who did, because from where I stand, you are in a heap of trouble, and I'm going to do everything I can to prove you're guilty. It sickens me that you're old enough to be her father and yet you still took advantage of her. A young girl who was your business partner's daughter."

The man's head popped up, his eyes wide. "I didn't have an affair with Tillie."

"And I'm supposed to believe you over the evidence we've collected."

"I'd never do that, Detective, because she's my daughter."

Oz straightened with the news. "Your daughter?"

"I've got the paternity test to prove it."

"Wait…so your affair was with Miranda Foxx? Your business partner's wife?"

The man gave a small nod. "And to answer your next question—he knows."

Oz stood, stunned at the revelation. Judd's information changed everything. Especially for Jeremiah Foxx.

TEN

Liz walked over to the precinct's tent where the body of Miranda Foxx rested and pulled back the sheet. The woman's eyes were closed and her face at peace. Unlike earlier in the day when she seemed agitated with Mayor DeMoss.

"What were you hiding?" Liz regretted not having more time to find out. With Tillie and her mother gone, all within less than a week, Liz connected the two crimes together even though the murderer had tried to make Miranda's death appear random with the active-shooter scenario. Now Liz needed to find the evidence to prove her theory.

A white van from the county office pulled up, and an older man stepped out from the driver's door with a digital tablet in hand.

Liz covered the woman's body again and stood. "I'm Detective Burke. I suppose you're here for the victim."

He tapped his screen. "Looks like there's two. Can you identify both of them and sign off for me."

"Two? Who's the second?" Liz took the tablet and scrolled down. Miranda was at the top of the list with a detailed summary of her death underneath, but the next name sent a chill up her spine. She looked up from the device and glanced behind her. Another white sheet fanned out, concealing the victim. His wheelchair sat nearby. She knelt to the ground and revealed his face. Instant tears blurred her vision.

"Did you know him, ma'am?" The coroner moved to her side.

She swiped her cheek. "Trey McManus."

Liz fought back the barrage of emotions swirling within her and pulled the sheet a bit lower. Blood soaked his shirt. One fatal wound to his chest. There was a time in her past where she'd prayed for his death, but now that his demise was a reality, she struggled. She'd loved him, but his abuse had changed her, cut away a part of who she was. Pieces of her soul gone forever.

"I'm so sorry for your loss, ma'am, and I hate to interrupt, but I need you to move away from the body. We have to do an autopsy on both the victims and need to preserve their remains."

She stood. "Did the police provide you with any details about his death?"

"Only where they found him. Looks like they recovered his body from the corner of Main and Sycamore Street."

"*I* was on Main and Sycamore. He must've been following me."

Trey didn't know Tillie or Miranda. She'd never introduced them. If the sniper hit him with a random shot, then his death was collateral damage. Unless she was missing something. As far as she could tell, there was only one common denominator between the three victims. *Her.*

The realization plagued her mind. She slipped around

the corner of a nearby building and leaned against the cold brick wall. What if she was the reason all three of them were dead?

Footsteps slapped the pavement behind her. "There you are." Oz's voice echoed between the buildings. "Have I got some—"

Without hesitation, Liz moved into his arms. "Trey's dead."

He paused, then tightened his arms around her. "I'm guessing he was shot?"

"A fatal wound to the chest."

Oz stepped back and retrieved his keys from his pocket. "Why don't I take you to the hotel?"

She shook her head. "We've got a job to do. I want to find who did this." The sobs returned.

"Liz. Come on. You're not going to be able to think straight until you've had some rest. To be honest, I'm pretty exhausted too, and my body aches. After the attack in the alley and the shooting today, no one would blame us for taking a small break. I'm sure Sergeant Wright will understand." She didn't want her grief to distract from finding the killer who continued to wreak havoc on their town. "Let's go to the precinct first. Jeremiah Foxx texted me, and I told him I would meet him there. He wants to talk about Miranda's death."

Oz led the way to his car. "I want to question Judd Thoreau too, and he's in a holding cell. We just need to make sure we keep them in separate areas of the precinct."

"They'll be in different rooms. Why do we need them to be in separate areas of the precinct?"

"Because Judd Thoreau didn't have an affair with Tillie, but with Jeremiah's wife, Miranda."

Liz halted her steps with the news. "What? I thought we had photos of Tillie at multiple restaurants across the town with Judd?"

Oz hit the button on his key fob to unlock the car doors. "She's his daughter."

"You've got to be kidding me."

"Can't make this stuff up."

Liz opened her door and slid into the passenger seat. "If Jeremiah knew that Miranda had an affair with Judd that produced a daughter—"

"That gives him motive to kill his wife and Tillie."

Could this entire case come down to a lover's quarrel and a jealous husband? She'd seen people carry out heinous crimes for a lot less. If so, then Trey was right when he said most murderers killed for one of three reasons: money, power or love. Liz just wasn't sure how her ex fit into that scenario.

The Mills Creek Police Department buzzed with energy from the aftermath of the festival. Detectives and officers scurried around and supplied information to concerned family members about loved ones who attended the festival. Thankfully, they had good news to share except for their two deceased victims.

After Liz talked with Oz regarding Judd Thoreau's testimony, she hoped the two cups of hot coffee and the homey setting of their soft interrogation room might help Jeremiah Foxx provide her with the truth.

He always seemed to be holding something back, covering for someone. Maybe he didn't want others to know about the affair or the damaged marriage he glossed over to keep up appearances, but with two murders so close to him, this was not the time for falsehoods. But if she pushed too hard too soon, then the man might lawyer up, and she'd never learn the truth.

Liz crossed the floor to where Jeremiah sat in one of the cushioned chairs, staring out the window. The image of a perfect grieving husband and father.

"Thought you could use a cup." She handed him the steaming beverage when he looked in her direction.

"Thank you, Detective." He wrapped his fingers around the outside, a gold wedding band present on his left hand.

"I'm so sorry about Miranda."

His eyes filled with tears. "I'm not sure what I'm going to do. I've lost both my girls. How did this happen?"

"For us to answer that, I need to ask you some difficult questions, but the more you can tell me, the easier we will be able to put the pieces together and get to the truth. These topics are sensitive in nature so please try not to take offense. They are standard questions we ask everyone going through similar situations. Any detail you can provide will help us find Miranda and Tillie's killer."

He took a sip and eyed her over the rim of his cup. "Of course. I'll answer whatever questions you have."

Liz retrieved the folder of photos Oz had given her earlier, then opened her laptop and pulled up the results of Judd's paternity test. She'd been able to track down the document with ease once she knew he was Tillie's father, but she held off on sharing the information.

"Did Miranda have anyone who wanted to harm her?" She left off the words *besides you* to ease him into the conversation and help him relax. Trust was the most important factor of the moment.

"Everyone loved my wife. She didn't have any enemies."

"So you think her death today was random?"

"Most likely. I suppose. Have we caught the shooter?"

"We're working on it, Mr. Foxx." Liz took a sip of her coffee. "Were you at the festival today? I didn't see you there."

"I wasn't able to attend because my son had a basketball game. Miranda and I decided a long time ago that at least one parent should be present at all our kids activities. I guess that will only be me now."

Liz jotted down a note to check the school's schedule and corroborate his alibi. "And he attends which high school?"

"Mills Creek Christian."

"Right." She kept her gaze on her notepad. "Did you know Tillie was not your biological daughter?"

Liz looked up as Jeremiah leaned back in the chair and tightened his fingers around the mug she'd given him. His discomfort was subtle, but she'd hit a nerve.

"I wondered when this news would finally come to light. If you're asking me about Judd and Miranda's affair, then yes, I know. Miranda came clean a couple of years ago after Tillie found out about her father. She promised me the affair ended long ago, but I must admit, Detective, I was devastated to find out Tillie was not my own. Even though Judd was her biological father, I never treated her any differently. I continued to love her like my own. Judd, on the other hand, didn't want to have anything to do with her."

"Until recently, correct?" Liz made a few notes.

"Not ever." The man shifted in his seat and took another sip of his coffee.

She reached into the folder and removed the images. "Then would you like to explain these photos of them together at one of your work parties?" She tapped the image of Judd. "That doesn't look like nothing to me. That looks like a man who wants to know his daughter."

"Still, he didn't support her financially or provide for her. Just swept in making empty promises. Judd failed her as a parent."

"And that upset you?"

"Tillie deserved better. He's the reason she left us. He's the reason she turned to drugs to find comfort. Very few girls can handle a father's rejection."

Tillie always carried an innate sadness within her. If what Jeremiah said was true, then Tillie had hoped to reconcile with her biological father, not Jeremiah. She never mentioned patching things up with her mother. But Jeremiah was wrong about one thing. From the evidence they'd collected, Judd had wanted to get to know Tillie.

She slid the receipt list across the table.

"What's this?" Jeremiah asked.

"All the items Mr. Thoreau purchased for his daughter, including the money for clothes and gas in her car. Maybe those promises weren't so empty, after all."

Jeremiah stared at the document. "I wasn't aware. That must've been after Tillie moved out."

"Not unusual for a teenage girl to keep secrets from her parents."

"I guess not."

"When did you find out that Miranda had renewed her affair with Judd?" Liz slid another image of Judd and Miranda huddled in a dark corner of a recent party.

"This image is from your recent fundraiser for Mayor DeMoss."

"They weren't together again, Detective. That image is two people trying to figure out the best way to get Tillie back on track. He said he had some connections and could get her a job after she worked off her hours of community service."

The answer made sense, and Liz didn't detect much jealousy in his tone. "When did Tillie find out about Judd being her father?"

"Right around her seventeenth birthday. She didn't take things well, and that's when she ran away. We searched for months and found her homeless on the street and paid to put her in rehab."

"And afterward, she returned home?"

"For a few weeks, but then after a relapse, her mother and I decided tough love was the best way to help her. We had to stop enabling her drug habit if we ever wanted Tillie to get clean for good. This time she voluntarily entered another treatment program. After about six months of therapy, and one halfway house, she got a small apartment in town. We thought she'd turned a corner and were all very grateful."

"How did you know of her whereabouts?"

"Friends kept tabs on her for us. We had connections and paid them to give us information. Also, Wendy helped."

"Mayor DeMoss?"

"She's a dear friend of ours. Wendy had one of her security team keep an eye on Tillie from time to time. Just to give us peace of mind that she wasn't returning to her old ways."

"Do you think Judd would harm Miranda or Tillie?"

"I won't pretend to know or understand any of Judd Thoreau's actions or lack thereof but if you're asking me do I think he's a killer, then no. I don't think so."

"Is there anyone you can think of that might've wanted to harm your wife and daughter?"

Jeremiah took another sip of his coffee and fought back tears. "I've run this scenario over in my head many times. My daughter got in with some rough people when she was doing drugs. We tried to help her, but she was stubborn. She also had a boyfriend who was a member of the East Mountain Mafia."

"Do you know his name?"

"I'll never forget it. Clive Hawkins."

Liz jotted down Clive's name. He'd been on the radar since the beginning of the case, but even if Clive had killed his girlfriend, why had he protected Liz while Miranda was shot at the festival? Unless his whole aim was to take out Tillie's mother.

Jeremiah gathered his coat. "If I've answered all your questions, I'd really like to get back to my son. He's not doing well with the death of his mother and sister."

"Of course. I'll call you if there's anything else I need." Liz escorted him to the door. "For what it's worth, Mr. Foxx, Tillie was trying to get her life straight and wanted to be reconciled with her family. She told me that on multiple occasions."

"So the rumors are true. Her service hours included working for you as an informant?"

"Her way of righting her wrongs."

Jeremiah nodded. "At least in the short time she was with us, she did some good with her life. Maybe some-one else's daughter will avoid a drug addiction because of her work. There is one more thing that keeps nagging at me about both of their deaths."

"What's that?"

"You."

Liz took a step back. "What do you mean?"

"When they both died, you were there, or at least in the vicinity. Maybe instead of focusing on Tillie's life, someone should look into yours. Were you really the intended target and my girls were simply in the wrong place at the wrong time? If I find out that's true, Detective, I can promise my lawyer will be in touch."

His insight twisted her gut. The thought had certainly crossed her mind, but she'd dismissed the notion as mere coincidence.

"And what about you, Mr. Foxx? Knowing about your wife's affair and your daughter's paternity gives you motive to kill them. Maybe you need to call your lawyer for your own benefit instead of being concerned about me."

"I would never kill my wife or daughter."

"We'll see where the evidence leads."

"I've got nothing to hide." He stepped through the door. "But if you do need to speak with me again, my legal team is Robin, Stevens and King." He handed her their card. "Here's their number."

The door clicked closed. Liz figured he had his lawyer on speed dial and would probably call him on the way to the elevator. She returned to her desk and pulled up Clive Hawkins in the national database and ran a background check. Mr. Foxx had been quick to point the finger at the EMM leader.

After collecting the man's rap sheet and all the financial records she could find, she spent the rest of the afternoon scrolling through mounds of paperwork. Clive's bank account held nothing exciting until the day of Tillie's death. A large sum had been deposited into his account. Now to track who sent the funds. One company popped up.

McManus Security.

Liz stared at the screen. Trey was dead, and she would be too if Clive hadn't protected her today. How did her ex figure into all of this? If he wanted her dead, then why wasn't there a bullet through her skull?

Oz entered the room. "You ready? I was thinking burgers from the Silver Spoon Café, then we can head to the hotel for some sleep."

"Trey paid Hawkins a large sum of money the day of Tillie's death." She kept scrolling. "We need to bring in Clive and find out why."

"I think we both know the reason why. You were his real target."

"Then why didn't he kill me the night he was in my apartment or the day we were on the train trestle or today at the fundraiser? Something else is going on, and I'm going to figure out who didn't want Trey and Miranda talking."

Liz snapped her laptop closed and grabbed her coat when she heard yelling from down the hall. She and Oz walked in that direction on their way out.

Wendy DeMoss paced back and forth, until Sergeant Wright ushered her into his office and closed the door. The automatic blinds flattened against his interior window. A clear sign her superior wanted no interruptions and an even better time for her and Oz to make an exit. From the volume of the mayor's voice echoing through the department, heads were gonna roll.

* * *

Oz opened the door of the hotel suite and wheeled in the room service cart the concierge left at their door. He removed the silver covers, checked the food and inhaled the grilled burger scent. "Dinner's here."

Liz emerged from her separate bedroom dressed in a gray lounge suit, little makeup and her hair in a ponytail. She lifted her meal and moved to the table. Oz grabbed a couple of waters from the mini fridge and handed her one.

"The hand-cut fries are really good," Liz said as she dipped one into a dollop of ketchup.

He followed suit and popped one into his mouth, not realizing how famished he was until he swallowed. If it were up to him, he'd order three more meals for himself alone, but since the sergeant was picking up their tab, he'd have to restrain his desires—something he'd been doing ever since this case started and Liz became his partner.

He finished off the burger and fought back a yawn. Not much longer and he'd have to turn in for the night. His energy level was exhausted, and he hoped he didn't end up like one of those toddlers on the internet who fall asleep at the kitchen table.

Liz pointed at the large-screen TV on the wall. "Can you turn that up?"

Oz moved his plate to the side, grabbed the remote and increased the volume. "Is that Mayor DeMoss?"

"Looks like she's holding a press conference about the shooting today. Too bad we aren't there in person."

"I don't want to be there in person. I'm perfectly content with a large-screen TV and a king-size bed calling my name."

Liz took a sip of her water. "Sounds like a plan to me. We can take a fresh look at the crime scene in the morning if you want."

Even with crews working around the clock to gather evidence, they wouldn't know much until the next day anyway. Clearing a crime scene took time, and their midsize department struggled to cover the crime and keep their regular tasks caught up. There was months of work ahead of them. Maybe years. At least their captain had called in reinforcements to help with the large area the shooting covered.

Oz propped his feet on a leather ottoman. "DeMoss sure is pretty adamant about catching whoever did this. And she's offering a twenty-five-thousand dollar reward for any information leading to the shooter."

"That will make someone a nice Christmas present." Liz took another bite of her burger. "She sure doesn't waste an opportunity to campaign, does she?"

Oz raised his water bottle toward the TV. "To a true politician."

"And she's pointing fingers at Clive and the East Mountain Mafia, which I have to say isn't a stretch."

"Didn't he protect you today?"

"Yeah. Doesn't mean he's not involved."

"Hard to be in two places at once."

"He's got minions that will blindly do whatever he tells them."

"True. I'll make sure I include that in my report to Sergeant Wright. I don't want them focusing on the wrong person while the other one is still out there planning the next attack."

Liz finished off her burger and wiped her mouth with a napkin. "I'm still baffled by it all really, and then with Trey's death… What a mess this all has turned out to be."

"Do you think Trey knew something we're missing?"

"Like what?"

"I'm not sure, but we've got three victims. Miranda, Trey and Tillie. Were they all working together? Did they know each other outside of this town? What's the common denominator?"

Liz tossed her napkin into the trash, hitting the basket with little effort. "Me."

He took the remote and muted the TV. "That's not what I meant."

"I know. But Jeremiah Foxx said something at the precinct that got me to thinking. I'm the common denominator. I was visiting Tillie when she was killed, and I was talking to Miranda when she got shot. Then when I talked with the coroner, he told me Trey was at the corner of Main and Sycamore when he was gunned down."

"How's that tied to you?"

"When Clive pulled me out from under the picnic table, we ran and hid at the corner of Main and Sycamore. Trey must've been following me."

"You think they orchestrated all this to abduct you from the scene?"

"Maybe. Although I'm more inclined to think he was protecting me."

"Let's walk through all the connections with Trey."

She dusted the salt from her fingertips and sat up straighter in the chair.

"The first time I saw Trey in years was the night he broke into my apartment. He didn't hurt me and said he came to make amends, which would explain what

Clive said on the trestle that someone wanted to talk to me. I think that was Trey. When I wouldn't go with Clive, Trey came to me, which explains why Clive protected me today. They must've seen the sniper."

"Which would mean the sniper was aiming for you and not Miranda."

Liz leaned back, quiet.

Breaking news scrolled across the bottom of the television set. East Mountain Mafia displayed all in capital letters. Oz unmuted the volume as Mayor DeMoss focused on the camera.

"Our evidence indicates the shooter was a member of the East Mountain Mafia, and if anyone has information on this group or their location, please contact the Mills Creek Police Department. We want justice served for the families affected by this unnecessary tragedy. This is law enforcement's top priority. We will not rest until we find the parties responsible."

Oz's phone buzzed with a message from Bronson. "Looks like the security footage of the shooting has been uploaded to our servers. I'll cast the video to the TV so we can both watch."

He hit Play on his phone and sat back. For a few moments at the beginning, people milled about the streets, content with shopping at booths and talking with friends. The temperatures were mild that day for December, and the sun was bright. Everyone seemed to be having a good time until gunfire interrupted the peace. Then chaos ensued.

"Looks like this is from the cameras located on the town hall building."

Liz leaned forward. "Can you go back?"

He rewound the footage, and she pointed at the

screen. "There. Crossing the street behind me. I thought I felt a push when I was running but didn't stop to look. Trey wheeled behind me and shoved me out of the way. That's when the sniper's bullet hit him."

Oz paused the scene. "He saved your life. If he hadn't shoved you, then the bullet would've hit you instead."

Liz rose from the table and turned her back to him. He clicked off the footage. "Are you okay?"

"How can I be? I've hated him for so long. Not just for the abuse but putting me in a position to shoot and paralyze him. The guilt has consumed me ever since that night. I wake up from horrible dreams." She motioned back to the television. "Now he dies saving my life. How am I supposed deal with that on top of everything else? It's my fault he couldn't walk, and now it's my fault he's dead."

"An assassin shot him. Not you."

"He wouldn't have even been in town if it weren't for me." Liz's phone buzzed on the counter, and she read the screen. Her face paled.

"What is it?"

"Clive Hawkins. He wants to meet with me down at the old rail yard. Says he has information about Trey's death."

She grabbed her coat and slipped on her boots discarded earlier by the door.

"I'm going too."

"I have to go alone."

Heat flushed into Oz's face. "Absolutely not. He tried to abduct you once when we were at the lake house. This could be a trap, and I'm not letting you go by yourself."

"He's not going to hurt me. That wasn't his objective." She pulled the zipper on her outer boot and straightened.

"Trey's dead and no longer giving Clive his orders. If there's one thing we know, it's that this man does whatever's necessary for a payday, and we don't know who's padding his pocket now."

"Fine. But stay out of sight. I have to find out what he knows about Trey, and I don't want him spooked. That's the least I can do for the man who saved my life."

"Then we want the same outcome." Oz didn't trust anyone at the moment, especially Clive Hawkins, who was at the top of his suspect list. The man was a paid assassin, and if this was his plan to finish the job, then he'd have to go through Oz first.

ELEVEN

Liz waited behind a shadowed column while keeping her eyes on the main opening. She never was a fan of the deserted rail yard. Too many drug deals and nefarious exchanges happened in the shadows of the covered pavilion. Plus, there were never enough places to hide if bullets started flying.

A figure topped a nearby hill and ran toward the structure. Clive walked underneath the covered roundhouse shelter, where trains used to enter for maintenance, and maneuvered around a large turntable. He stepped to the center and turned in a circle, scanning the outer perimeter. She kept her presence hidden.

Oz spoke into her comms device he required her to wear. "He's clean. I don't see any weapons."

He'd insisted on being nearby with a sniper rifle topped with a night vision scope. She had to admit, having him close and knowing he was armed kept her relaxed.

Liz stepped into view. "I'm here."

With a startled turn, Clive faced her, a look of fear in his eyes. "Thanks for coming."

"You said you had information about Trey's death. What do you know?"

The man looked freaked. He shifted his weight from one foot to the other and flinched at every little noise. His eyes darted around, only landing on her when needed. "They're going to kill me. I know too much."

"Who's going to kill you?"

Any trace of his confident bravado demonstrated on the train tracks had vanished. She needed to reassure him, calm him down so he would talk. Probably didn't help he was a sitting duck out in the open.

"Step over here, next to this wall so you're not exposed. Then you can tell me."

Static filtered through her earpiece. "I thought we agreed you'd keep your distance."

She looked to Oz's location with his scope aimed right on her. "Not my first time."

"What did you say?" Clive looked back over his shoulder.

Liz forced a small smile to her face. "This is not my first time coming to the roundhouse. My uncle used to work here. He drove a train and one time let me climb up in the engine and pull the horn."

Clive moved closer and leaned against the wall. "I lived in an abandoned railcar once. For a couple of months. Winter set in, and my mom moved us to our uncle's house. Biggest mistake of our lives, but we had heat. I promised my momma when I got big, I'd take care of her one way or another. And I have."

Liz let a silent moment pass between them. Nice to know the man cared about his mother. Didn't excuse the criminal acts he committed to keep his vows, but the idea that Clive had a heart was a tidbit of psychology she could use.

"Do you protect her like you protected me?"

He ran a hand over his stubbled beard. "I guess I have a soft spot for damsels in distress. Call me old-fashioned."

If only he knew the defensive training she had, he wouldn't think her so weak. "I know Trey paid for my protection. Is that why someone wants you dead?"

"When he first came to me, he wanted me to find you and convince you to talk to him. Later on is when he paid me more to protect you."

"He didn't hire you to kill me?"

A shocked look crossed the man's face. "Not at all. In fact, he was adamant we do everything to keep you alive. You didn't make the job easy though."

Nothing about her relationship with Trey had ever been easy. "Why did he think my life was in danger?"

"Because of the professional hit on you."

"Someone wanted me dead?"

"Apparently, you were a little too good at your narcotics job and got in the way of their drug trafficking. That's why they took out Tillie. She was your informant."

"What about Miranda?"

"I'm not sure why they killed her, but he had proof about the hit on your life."

"Did he show you that proof?"

"Nope. The less I knew the better. He wanted me to keep you safe and that's what we did."

Liz paced between the columns, trying to make sense of it all. "How'd he find out about the hit?"

"Through his security connections. I guess after you moved here, he kept tabs on you through his massive network. Plus, he was friends with Judd and Miranda. They'd go out to dinner and such. He didn't know Miranda was married and thought the two of them made a nice couple. Often reminisced about his time with you."

"He ruined that."

"Whatever happened between the two of you is none of my concern. After Trey heard about the threat on your life, he came to town under the guise of opening a satellite office."

"Did he happen to say who hired the assassin?"

"He was trying to figure out their identity, but he did talk about an alliance several key business leaders put together as a way to control the town's industry."

Something scuffed behind them, and Clive pulled her behind one of the columns. "This is not a good spot. We're too open here."

"Were you followed?"

"Not that I saw."

A cat meowed from the corner and raced after a nighttime critter. Liz pulled away from his grip. "I think we're fine." She brushed dirt from her jacket sleeve. "Did Jeremiah Foxx happen to be a part of this alliance?"

"Y'all need to get out of there," Oz said through her comms device. "I see movement at three o'clock. Someone else is—"

Shots rang out, and Clive grabbed his upper thigh, blood dripping through his fingers. Liz pulled him back around the side of the column and retrieved her gun. "Oz, have you got a visual on the shooter?"

"Yeah. I'll cover you. Run for the SUV."

"Someone's with you?" Clive asked. "I should've known this was a setup."

"This is not a setup. He's our protection."

Oz returned fire as Liz struggled to help Clive into

the back seat of the vehicle. Once inside, she dug out a towel from the console and tossed it to Clive before hopping into the driver's seat. Gunfire erupted around the outer perimeter of the car. "Put pressure on your wound."

Liz shifted into Drive, picked up Oz and swerved onto the road leading away from the rail yard.

She glanced in the rearview mirror. "Is he okay? He took a bullet to the thigh."

"He needs a hospital."

"Can you tell if he has a graze or if the bullet is lodged?"

"It's lodged."

She pressed the gas pedal to the floor, and Oz grabbed the back of her seat. "Take a left. There's a shortcut on McDowell Street that will get you closer to the emergency room entrance."

Two black sedans whipped out onto the road and gained ground. Liz swerved onto the side road and kept a decent distance. More gunfire erupted. The back glass shattered. Oz placed a call to Dispatch and requested backup.

"These guys don't give up do they?" Liz asked.

"Clive, if you have any idea who's behind us, now would be a good time for that info."

"I can promise you this. None of my guys are involved."

Liz took a hard left into the entrance of the hospital, and Clive released a groan.

"Almost there, Hawkins. Hang on."

"You can't stop for me. A hospital won't keep them from coming after you."

Liz glanced in the rearview mirror again. "What if I drop you off and keep going?"

"That would be best."

"Before we do, tell me who the members of the alliance are. One of these people could be behind all of this."

His breaths grew more labored as Liz sped over a speed bump. "Foxx, Thoreau, McManus and Mayor DeMoss are the only ones I know about, even though I'm pretty sure there's a few more members."

"Thanks." She stopped in front of the emergency room doors, and Oz helped Clive out. The man groaned in pain. "You're going to have to help him inside. I'll wait for you right up there at the end of the portico."

Oz didn't hesitate and supported the man as he hobbled through the automatic doors. Tires squealed into the entrance and Liz shifted into Drive. Before she could pull into the road, a navy blue sedan moved in front of her car from a side street, blocking her exit. Oz was nowhere in sight.

She revved the gas, ready to smash into the vehicle if needed to escape, but the sedan's back passenger door opened. A woman stepped into view with a tall man behind her, gun to her head. Fear was etched across the woman's face. *Mayor Wendy DeMoss.*

Her phone rang and Liz answered. There was only one option.

Surrender and go with them to save the mayor's life.

Oz stepped from the hospital as a navy blue sedan peeled into the main road. He ran to the SUV, still running in the lane. Liz's gun and cell phone remained on the driver's seat.

He jumped inside and took off after them, winding through back roads and trying keep them in his sight. They turned onto Main Street.

Oz circled the block and slowed his speed. They had to be here somewhere. He turned down Sycamore Street and made another lap, scanning the tall buildings lining the road. Most of the businesses were dark at one in the morning, but when a small third-floor window on the back side of town hall flicked to life, he knew the timing was too coincidental.

He parked across the street, pulled his weapon and slipped into the garage located underneath. A navy sedan sat in a space near the stairwell entrance but no one was inside. He moved to the door and tried the handle. Locked, and a black box entry code was required.

With time against him, Oz ran to the other three outside doors but found all of them secured for the night. He had to get into the building—the same building he and Liz climbed yesterday. He'd made the ascent all the way to the roof with Liz by his side. But she wasn't with him this time.

He shifted his gaze to the fire escape. If he wanted to save Liz's life, he'd climb the ladder again.

Oz reached up and pulled the first section to the ground, then gripped the bars of each rung. Rusted metal bit into his fingers but he made his ascent. With one glance to the street, his head swirled.

"Don't look down," he said in an effort to pep up his courage.

Didn't work. Those same people who rattled off the trite statement scaled mountains and waterfalls, oblivious to the fear trying to incapacitate him in midair.

Frigid wind blew and numbed his fingered grip on the second set. The higher he climbed, the harder his heart pumped and the shorter his breaths became. Once on the second-story landing, he leaned against the building, willing himself to take the last flight to the window.

Shadows moved behind the glow, and he could hear people talking. He placed his foot on the next rung and lifted his body closer to the glass. A woman's voice rose in volume. He'd heard that voice before, shouting at his sergeant. *Mayor DeMoss.*

Oz stepped onto the third-floor landing and peeked inside. Shelves of labeled office supplies lined the walls. Boxes of printer paper, ink cartridges and old laptops covered tables in the middle of the floor. Liz sat in a leather chair with one large man behind her.

Mayor DeMoss paced around her, gun in hand.

"I can't believe I fell for your ruse." Liz raised her chin in defiance. "You never were his hostage, were you?"

"Thanks for finally joining the party," the woman said.

"What about the fundraiser? Was that all a ploy too?"

Oz tried to lift the window so he could hear better, but the pane wouldn't budge. The mayor took a seat across from Liz. "More like a setup. The perfect opportunity to take out a few people who'd uncovered my little secrets."

"Like Trey and Miranda."

"You just couldn't leave well enough alone, could you? Always having to uncover the truth. Well, now you have it, Detective. I hope you're satisfied."

"*You* were behind the sniper?"

Oz tightened his grip on his gun. He'd take the woman out if he had a clean shot, but he might hit Liz from this angle.

"That's all on you. Arresting all my contacts and

shutting down my lines of trade. Then your little ex-boyfriend shows up, and he runs surveillance on me. He uncovered our operation within a week. If only I could've convinced him to work with me, but he wouldn't budge unless you joined the team. I knew you wouldn't run drugs with your righteous mindset so—"

"That's why you wanted me on your security team."

Wendy stood again and paced. "Figured if I had you under my thumb, I could keep you from shutting down more of my drug network, but when you refused, I had to stop you. Trey wasn't happy with my decision."

"And Tillie. Why'd you kill her? She was an innocent girl."

The mayor let out a laugh. "Innocent? Hardly. She was one of my best dealers until you took her from me."

The mayor pressed the barrel of her gun to Liz's head, and Oz raised his weapon. He'd have to shoot through the glass and prayed the only person he injured was DeMoss.

"This drug operation is mine, and ever since you arrived in town, you've interfered, and I don't like it when detectives and their confidential informants get in my way."

The large man hit Liz across the cheek at Wendy's signal. If Oz didn't get inside, they'd kill her for sure. He grabbed the ladder to his right and climbed to the roof, running across to the clock tower. He pulled on the door, which opened, and raced down the stairs until he reached the room. A sliver of light brushed across the hallway. He slipped inside, remaining in the shadows.

"What about Miranda?"

"That bullet was meant for you. We missed."

Oz stepped around a stack of boxes and aimed at the

mayor's head. "Wendy, put down your gun. You're under arrest for the murder of Tillie Foxx, Miranda Foxx and Trey McManus."

The woman pressed the gun to Liz's head. "I'll kill her if you come one step closer."

Oz's heart raced, but he knew he had no choice. This woman had taken too many lives already. "Step away and I won't hurt you."

Wendy smirked. "Kelly? Isn't that your last name?"

"Put the weapon down."

"I knew your brother. He was one of my best clients. Pity what he did to your wife."

Heat rushed through him, and he fought to maintain control of his rage.

"The boy loved heroin. Couldn't get enough of it. He's in the state penitentiary, right? I've got some connections on the inside. I'll have to reach out to them on his behalf."

Oz restrained himself from pulling the trigger at her threat, holding back all the hatred and anger flowing through his veins. A strong arm knocked the gun from his hand, whipped him into a muscled choke hold and dragged him across the floor. The guard pushed him to his knees in front of the mayor, where she turned the gun on him.

"Don't," Liz said.

Wendy narrowed her gaze. "I'll let him live, but you have to join me and keep your fellow cops out of my way. Remember, I said I'd triple your salary, but since you've put me in such a predicament, maybe we'll only double it instead."

Oz couldn't let Liz make a huge mistake by working for the mayor's organization. "Don't you dare."

Liz leaned forward in her chair. "How many times do I have to tell you, I'm capable of making my own decisions, Oz, and if working for her saves your life, then so be it."

She gave him a covert wink before she straightened, keeping her body a bit closer to her adversary. Liz held out her hand to the mayor. "You've got a deal."

Wendy looked at her, shifting her attention from Oz, and Liz lunged for her gun and knocked the mayor to the floor. The guard stepped in to break up the fight, but Oz pulled his ankle weapon and aimed it at the man's head. "Don't even think about it."

The man paused and raised his hands in the air.

"It's over, Wendy," Oz said. "Give yourself up."

She continued to wrestle Liz for control of the weapon and didn't respond. Liz lost her balance and both fell to the ground. One shot fired.

Liz pushed the mayor off her body to assess the injury. She pressed her hands to the wound low in the abdomen. Wendy was losing blood fast.

Oz grabbed a nearby blanket and tossed it to her. She replaced her hands with the fabric, holding it to the area. Memories of the night she shot Trey rushed back with a vengeance. Same area. Same blank look in his eyes. *Please, God, don't let her die.*

Panic filled Wendy's face and Liz tried to keep her calm. "We're going to get you to the hospital. Stay with me, okay?" She turned to Oz. "Call 911."

He complied. "Ambulance is on its way."

"She's losing a lot of blood. We can't let her die."

"Here, let me help." He knelt beside Liz and placed his hands over hers, adding more pressure.

"Dear Jesus. Please—" Liz couldn't finish the prayer. This was all her fault. Her punishment for past sins. "Don't let her die."

A sense of peace flushed through her despite the chaos of the moment. The kind that didn't make sense in the midst of tragedy. She'd always feared the dark moments of her life, the hidden places and locked closets of fear, but every time despair reared its ugly head, a supernatural steadiness flooded her soul.

Sirens blared in the distance.

The color in Mayor DeMoss's face paled, and the woman's eyes tracked to Liz's gaze but rolled as she lost consciousness.

Within seconds, paramedics pushed into the room and hooked up an IV while another provided life-giving measures to keep Wendy alive. Liz followed them down the stairs and out the door. Red emergency lights lit up the street with their departure.

She took a seat on the wide stone steps leading up to the entrance of the town hall building, dangling her stained hands over her knees.

"You okay?" Oz joined her.

"I will be if she lives to face the charges."

"At least we know who was behind the killings now."

"And we have justice for Tillie, Miranda and Trey."

He brushed against her shoulder. "Don't be so sure about that. She's got a team of lawyers that will most likely get her off."

"Then we have to build a strong case so that doesn't happen."

"We will."

Oz helped her to her feet and back into the building. Liz followed him down the hall and into one of the bathrooms. He turned on the warm water, took her hands in his and washed the bloodstains from her skin.

He moved without saying a word, dried her hands, then dampened some paper towels and brushed them against her forehead, his gaze holding hers. "I'm glad you're okay."

"Thanks." She didn't back away. The nearness of him pulsed through her. Everything about him drew her closer—his spice-scented cologne, the longing in his eyes, the gentle touch still caressing her face. His soft lips moved to hers and she responded, letting his love erase the pain of her past. Forever.

Oz walked through his front yard a week after Christmas and pulled the plugs on the Christmas inflatables, watching each one of the characters collapse. The holidays were over, and according to social tradition and his neighbors, the time had come to remove all his decorations. The rest of winter always seemed a little bleaker once Santa's reindeer went back into the shed.

He flipped on the power switch one last time and stood on the sidewalk as the sun descended behind the mountains, letting the colorful scene transport him back to a time when his brother was well and everyone was happy. He pulled the stamped letter from his jacket pocket and ran his thumb across Clay's name. He might not be ready to visit in person, but he hoped his letter brought his little brother a bit of New Year cheer.

"I believe you owe me a rain check." Liz's voice interrupted the moment, and Oz turned to find her standing behind him.

He tucked the letter away and held out his arms. "Here? Now?"

"I've never danced in the middle of Christmas lights before, and this just happens to be my favorite song."

"Silent Night" played through the speaker. Oz reached out, took Liz's hand and pulled her into his arms. She wore her own clothes tonight—a long white coat, brown boots and a green beret that matched her eyes.

Her fingers brushed against his cheek. "Why haven't you called or come by to see me? I've missed you."

Oz shrugged. "I wanted to give you some much needed downtime with your father for Christmas. Plus, after the case was over, there was so much publicity and press. You were the highlight of the department, and I wasn't sure you wanted me to cross our professional line."

Liz stopped moving and dragged her boot heel through the snow. "This line?"

He smiled. "Cute."

She sashayed out of his arms and stepped across to the other side, then held out her hand to him. "The risk is up to you."

For the first time in five years, Oz didn't care about being cautious or following the rules. All he wanted was her. With one stride, he chose a fresh start.

"I love you, Detective Liz Burke."

She held his gaze for a moment, returned the words he longed to hear and met his lips—warm and sweet, with a slight taste of peppermint. The perfect gift for Christmas.

* * * * *

If you liked this story from Shannon Redmon,
check out her previous
Love Inspired Suspense books,

Cave of Secrets
Secrets Left Behind
Mistaken Mountain Abduction

Available now from Love Inspired Suspense!
Find more great reads at www.LoveInspired.com.

Dear Reader,

Thank you for reading Oz and Liz's story. Every time I research law enforcement, I'm amazed at the sacrifice these men and women make to keep us safe each day. These officers aren't perfect, as we see reflected in our hero and heroine, but most of them hold a high regard for truth and justice. They experience the worst evils in our society while held to the highest standards for every decision they make. When we support them, our cities and neighborhoods are more peaceful. Without our officers, chaos and lawlessness ensue. My prayer is wisdom and safety for them as they do their jobs.

As always, I love hearing from readers. Contact me through my website, shannonredmon.com, or email me at shannon@shannonredmon.com. I'm happy to answer any writing questions you have. Also, you can find me on Goodreads, BookBub and all other social media platforms.

Blessings,
Shannon Redmon

HARLEQUIN
PLUS

Try the best multimedia
subscription service for romance
readers like you!

Read, Watch and Play.

Experience the easiest way to get
the romance content you crave.

Start your **FREE TRIAL** at
<u>www.harlequinplus.com/freetrial</u>.